# SALVATION

---

## AN ASH PARK NOVEL

### MEGHAN O'FLYNN

SALVATION

Copyright 2018

This is a work of fiction. Names, characters, businesses, places, events and incidents are either the products of the author's imagination or used fictitiously. Any resemblance to actual persons, living or dead, or actual events is purely coincidental. Opinions expressed are those of the characters and do not necessarily reflect those of the author, though she's at least 85.54% as leery of authority as Detective Petrosky.

No part of this book may be reproduced, stored in a retrieval system, scanned, or transmitted or distributed in any form or by any means electronic, mechanical, photocopied, recorded or otherwise without written consent of the author. Deferring to the proper authorities on this one is critical. Even Detective Petrosky would listen.

All rights reserved, including the right to send Detective Petrosky after anyone who doesn't abide by applicable copyright laws.

Distributed by Pygmalion Publishing, LLC

*For my family,
who saves me every day.*

**1**

———

*THE FUCK you want to be, boy?*

The drill sergeant's voice rang in Edward Petrosky's head, though it had been two years since he'd left the army, and six years since he'd had the question barked at him. Back then, the answer had been different. Even a year ago, he would have said "a cop," but that was more because it felt like an escape from the military, just like the Gulf War had been an escape from the loaded silence of his parents' house. But the urge to escape had passed. Now he would have said "Happy, sir," without a trace of irony. The future was shaping up to be good; better than the early nineties or the eighties, that was for damn sure.

Because of *her*.

Ed had met Heather six months before, in the spring before his twenty-fifth birthday, when the air in Ash Park still smelled like earthen death. Now he rolled over on the purple sheets she'd called "plum" and wrapped an arm over her shoulders, his gaze on the popcorn ceiling. A tiny half-smile played on her face with a strange twitch at one corner, almost a spasm, like her lips weren't sure whether to smile or frown. But the corners of her still-closed eyes were crinkled —definitely a smile. *Screw going out running.* The night he met her, she'd smiled like that. Barely forty degrees outside and she'd been taking off her leather coat, and by the time he rolled to a stop, she'd had the jacket wrapped around the homeless woman sitting on the walk. His last girlfriend used to stuff extra garlic bread in her purse when they went out to eat but refused to give even a quarter to the hungry, citing the degenerates' "lack of willpower." As if anyone would choose to starve.

Heather would never say something like that. Her breath was hot against his shoulder. Would his parents like her? He imagined driving the thirty minutes to Grosse Pointe for Thanksgiving next week, imagined sitting at their antique dining table, the one with the lace tablecloth that covered all the scars. "This is Heather," he'd say, and his father would nod, impassive, while his mother stiffly offered coffee, her steel-blue eyes silently judging, her lips pressed into a tight, bloodless line. His parents would ask thinly veiled questions, hoping Heather came from money—she didn't—hoping she'd make a good housewife or that she had dreams of becoming a teacher; of course, only until she bore his children. Dark ages shit. His parents didn't even like Hendrix, and that was saying something. You could get a read on anyone by asking their opinion on Jimi.

Ed planned to tell his folks Heather was self-employed and leave it at that. He'd not mention that he met her during a prostitution sting, or that the first bracelet he put on her wrist was made of steel. Some might argue that the start of a great love story couldn't possibly involve prostitution and near-hypothermia, but they'd be wrong.

Besides, if he hadn't put Heather in his squad car, one of the other units would have. Another time, another girl, he might have responded differently, but she'd been sniffling, crying so hard he could hear her teeth chattering. "You okay?" he had asked. "Do you need a drink of water or a tissue?" But when he glanced in the rearview of the squad car, her cheeks had been wet, her hands frantically rubbing her arms, and he'd realized her shaking was more from the cold.

Heather stretched now with a noise that was half groan, half meow, and snuggled farther under the covers. Ed smiled, letting his gaze drift past her shoulder and to his uniform on the chair in the corner. He still couldn't believe he'd uncuffed her in the supercenter parking lot and then left her sitting in the heated car while he headed into the store alone. When he came back with a thick yellow coat, her eyes had filled, and she'd smiled at him again in a way that made his heart feel four sizes bigger, made him feel taller like he was a hero and not the man who'd just tried to arrest her. They'd talked for hours after that, her whispering at first and looking out the windows like she could get in trouble just for speaking. She hadn't told him then that she hated yellow—he'd found out later. Not like there'd been a ton of options at that off-the-freeway supercenter anyway.

Ed let his vision relax, his black uniform blurring against the chair. Heather had told him she'd never talked to anyone that way before, so open, so easily, like they'd known each other forever. Then again, she'd also said it was the first time she'd ever walked the streets; the odds of that were slim, but Ed didn't care. If a person's past defined them, then he was a murderer; killing someone during wartime didn't make them any less dead. He and Heather were both starting over.

Heather moaned gently again and shifted closer to him, her light eyes hooded in the dimness. He brushed away the single mahogany tendril plastered to her forehead, accidentally snagging his calloused finger on the corner of the notebook under her pillow—she must have stayed up writing notes about the wedding again.

"Thanks for going with me yesterday," she whispered, her voice husky with sleep.

"No problem." They'd taken her father, Donald, to the grocery store, Donald's gnarled fingers shaking every time Ed looked down at the wheelchair. Congestive heart failure, arthritis—the man was a mess, hadn't been able to walk more than a few feet for over a decade, and by all accounts, shouldn't be alive now; usually, congestive heart failure took out its victims within five years. One more reason to get out of the house and enjoy each day, Heather always said. And they'd tried, even taken her father to the dog park, where the old man's miniature Doberman pinscher had yapped and run around Ed's ankles until Ed picked him up and scratched his fuzzy head.

He lowered himself to the pillow beside her, and she trailed her fingers over the hard muscles of his arm and across his chest, then nestled her head into his neck. Her hair still smelled like incense from church last night: spicy and sweet with the bitter hint of char over the gardenia shampoo she used. The church services and Donald's weekly bingo game were the only outings that Petrosky begged off. Something about that church bothered Ed. His own family wasn't particularly religious, but he didn't think that was the problem; maybe it was how the pope wore fancy hats and golden briefs, while less fortunate folks starved. At least Father Norman, Heather's priest, gave as well as he got. Two weeks before, Petrosky and Heather had taken three garbage bags of clothes and shoes the father had collected to the homeless shelter where Heather volunteered. Then they'd made love in the newly empty back seat of his car. What woman could resist an old Grand Am with squealing brakes and an interior that stank of exhaust?

Heather kissed his neck just below his ear and sighed. "Daddy loves you, you know," she said. Her voice had the same raspy quality as the frigid autumn air that rustled the branches outside.

"Eh, he just thinks I'm a good guy because I volunteer at the shelter." Which Ed didn't. But weeks before Ed met the man, Heather told her dad that she and Ed worked at the shelter together, and even after he and Donald were introduced, she hadn't told her father they were dating. He could understand that though—the man was strict, especially about his only daughter, another parent from the "spare the rod, spoil the child" era. Like Ed's own father.

A curl fell into her eye, and she blew it away. "He thinks you guys have a lot in common."

Donald and Ed spent most of their time together talking about their posts in Vietnam and Kuwait, respectively, but they'd never discussed exactly what they'd done. Ed assumed this was another reason Donald liked Father Norman; the priest had been a soldier before he joined up with the church, and nothing turned men into brothers like the horrors of the battlefield. "I like your father too. And the offer is still open: if he needs a place to stay, we can take care of him here."

She shifted her weight, and gardenia and incense wafted into his nostrils again. "I know, and you're sweet for offering, but we don't need to do that."

But they would, eventually. Unease prickled deep in the back of Ed's brain, a little icicle of frost that spread down into the marrow of his spine. Donald had worked at the post office after the war, through Heather's early childhood, and through his wife's suicide, but his heart had put him out of commission when Heather was a teenager. The man had squirreled some money away, but if Heather had been desperate enough to sell her body, Donald's carefully laid nest egg must have been running out. "Heather, we might—"

"He'll be fine. I've been saving since my mom died, just in case. He has more than enough to support him until he...goes."

*If she has all this money, why go out on the street?* "But—"

She covered his mouth with hers, and he put his hand on her lower back and pulled her tighter against him. Was living in his own place her father's way to maintain independence? Or was it Heather's? Either way, intuition told him not to push it, and the military had taught him to listen to his gut. Her father was one subject Heather rarely broached. Probably why Ed hadn't known his relationship with Heather was a secret...until he'd let it slip. And the next day, he'd come home from work, and Heather's things were in his bedroom. *It's perfect for us, Ed. Can I stay?*

*Forever*, he'd said. *Forever*.

Were they moving too fast? He wasn't complaining, didn't want some long, drawn-out courtship, but it had only been six months, and he never wanted Heather to give him the same look his mother always gave his father: *God, why are you still alive? Go ahead and die already so I can have a few happy years alone before I kick off.*

"Are you happy here?" he asked her. "With me?" Maybe they should slow things down just a little. But Heather smiled in that twitchy, spastic way of hers, and his chest warmed, the icicle in his spine melting. He was sure. His gut said, "For god's sake, marry her already."

"Happier than I've ever been," she said.

Ed kissed the top of her head, and as she arched against him, he smiled in the subtle gray of the dawn. Everything smelled sweeter when you were twenty-five and done with active duty in the sand, when every path was still yours for the taking. He'd seen some shit, god knew he had, and it still came to him at night: the horror of comrades shot dead beside him, the burning smog of gunpowder in the air, the tang of blood. But all that seemed so damn far away these days, as if coming home had turned him into someone else, someone who'd never been a soldier at all—all that military shit was someone else's baggage.

He traced the gentle curve of Heather's spine and let the porcelain sheen of her skin in the dusky morning erase the last remnants of memory. Even with the streets covered in slush that froze your toes the moment you stepped outside, her smile—that quirky little smile—always warmed him up.

Yes, this year was going to be the best of Ed's life. He could feel it.

2

Ed lit a cigarette and blew smoke out the frosty window, cracked open though it was colder than a yeti's balls. Patrick O'Malley frowned at him anyway, black brows drawn together in the center of his flat forehead. Ed had always thought Irish people were gingers, but this one came with hair and eyes darker than the Italians.

"You going to bitch at me about the smoke again?" Ed muttered.

"Not today," Patrick told the windshield, scratching his temple where the tiniest peppering of gray streaked the hair near the brim of his department-issued hat. "I'll wait until tomorrow to tell ye how you're like to die of lung cancer."

"The doctors told my mom to smoke when she was pregnant because it was good for her." Ed inhaled more deeply on the cig. Something about keeping her weight down, though his mother had still proclaimed her distaste for *his* smoking, and unlike Patrick, she'd said it in a way that made Ed feel guilty instead of defensive. Mothers were good at guilt without even trying—how could you ever repay a woman for squeezing your fat, squalling ass into existence?

"Healthy smoking is rare as hen's teeth."

*Fucking Irishman.* But Ed was all muscle beneath his policeman's uniform, and he ran an hour almost every morning without losing his air—until he stopped being able to do that, he'd pass on rethinking his tobacco habit. "I'll show you hen's teeth." He blew a lungful of smoke into Patrick's face, and the man squinted, frowned, and rolled down his window.

"You can kill yerself all ye like, but don't take me with ye!" Patrick sniffed hard and wiped the tiny smudge of white powder from beneath one nostril. Ed looked away. Blow had never stopped Patrick from doing his job, and half the soldiers stationed with Ed overseas wouldn't have been able to cope if they hadn't been riding a needle at night.

"You'll be fine, Paddy."

"It's not about me. Your new coat's going to smell like shite, and ye spent a fuckin' hour picking it out."

Ed glanced at the bag on the empty back seat behind him —he'd wanted to bring the jacket to lunch with them this afternoon. And in his head, he could hear Heather's father: "Where'd you get that coat anyway? I thought you hated yellow."

She'd blushed enough that Ed had known it must be true. But purple…she loved purple. He wasn't sure about style, but a coat was a coat, right? *Maybe she cried when you gave her the first one because it was just that fucking bad.* She'd called it her "favorite lemon" after he'd found out about her hatred of the color. Now Ed always ordered lemons in his water, just to make her lip twitch.

"The coat'll be fine too." He faced front again and stared out the window, looking left then right for broken taillights and speeders, but saw only the snow mounded against the curbs and one lone mitten lying frozen on the walk. How did Patrick do this year after year? The man had been on the beat when Ed was still in middle school. But ol' Paddy might be sick of it too; at the station, they called him "Stone Balls" after the name of some cannon—a loose cannon—though the Irishman was still friendly enough with the brass to get away with lost paperwork or perps who whined Paddy'd cuffed them too tight. Ed sighed a tobacco-laden cloud into the chill air and closed the window just as the tires kicked up slush from the gutter, spattering stained snow against the window. Nasty day. And it was about to get nastier. Maybe.

Ed cleared his throat. "We're going to that greasy spoon on Gratiot later," he said, and Patrick frowned until Ed finished: "Heather will be there."

Now Ed's partner raised an eyebrow. "I finally get to meet yer girl, eh?"

Ed nodded instead of answering—his mouth had gone too dry to speak. *We should wait.* He hadn't even bought a ring yet, but Donald had stared at him so hard the night they told him she was moving out that Ed had proposed the moment they were alone again. Guy was probably pissed as hell they'd moved in together without saying their vows first under God, but Donald, of all people, knew good love stories weren't perfect at the beginning...or the end. Heather's biggest fear was winding up like her mother, with a gun in her hand and a bullet in her brain. But this story wouldn't end that way.

Patrick smiled, a lopsided grin Ed thought of as Irish smug. "'Bout damn time I get to meet the woman you've been hiding."

Ed's stomach soured. *I should have told him about Heather before, come clean about the streetwalking thing.* No, there was no point in embarrassing her unnecessarily, and she had no criminal record—Patrick would have no idea of her history. She said she'd only walked the streets once, anyhow. But would that make a difference to his partner? Or the fact that

Heather had been on her high school track team, that she'd been a straight-A student, that she volunteered hours of her time every week at the shelter? Every woman Patrick picked up during that sting had ended up in a cell—Patrick's holier than thou Irish-Catholic ass would have something to say about the fact that Heather'd been a—

The radio squawked; ten-fifty-six. Intoxicated pedestrian. Patrick stopped at a light—this call too lame even to necessitate the siren—and Ed watched an abandoned plastic bag whirl through the cold gray air and land on a snowdrift. He sighed again. "If you could be anything..." Heather had asked him the night they met, her eyes gleaming in the brilliant white light from the supercenter parking lot. "I mean...do you think you'll be a cop forever?"

No, he didn't, but he had never said that out loud before—to anyone. "I'm a pretty good shot," he'd told her. "Maybe the academy will let me teach one day." And after a pause, he'd asked her, too: "What do you want to do with the rest of your life?"

"I've always loved animals. Maybe I'll be a vet. Or run a zoo. Breed doves." And he could see it, the doves, see her sitting on a park bench grinning that twitchy little smile while the birds flocked around her. Like Mary freaking Poppins, but cuter.

Ed crossed his arms against his washboard stomach, watching the slush through the passenger window. Shit, he should become one of those fitness trainers instead—pancakes every morning was how his grandmother went out. Heart attack at fifty-five. Damn shame. At fifty-five, he'd be drinking coffee in his dining room in some good-for-kids neighborhood, Heather's lip twitching up at him over a table without a lace tablecloth or any other covering because they'd accept things for what they were, scars and all. Maybe he and Heather would be grilling their own son's new girlfriend about what she wanted to be when she grew up. Ed liked to think he and Heather would just offer their child's love interest a drink and not be dicks about it, but he'd definitely ask whether she liked Hendrix. Sometimes the answer to one question was all you needed.

**3**
_______

PATRICK YANKED at the door handle, and a blast of stale heat from inside the restaurant slapped Ed in the face along with the delightful stink of frying bacon fat. He kept his eyes forward and not on his partner. And squared his shoulders. If Patrick did recognize her…well, it wasn't illegal to marry a woman with a sketchy past, and that's just what he'd say if anyone tried to give him shit.

"So, where is she?"

Ed glanced around. A pair of truckers sat in the back, one staring out the window smoking a cigarette, the other hunched over his plate in the protective way of an ex-con as he shoveled chili fries into his mouth. Two older women sat in the other booth, each boasting tight curls with a bluish tint —must have come straight from the salon.

Ed gestured to the closest blue-haired woman. "There she is, the one on the right," he said, then waved when the women glanced in his direction.

Patrick snorted. "Ye scoundrel."

Ed turned to the other side of the restaurant—*there*. She was at the table in the far corner, her bright yellow back to him and Patrick, her shoulders slumped. The coat was a little gaudy, now that he really looked at it. He gripped the department store bag tighter.

Heather turned as they approached, and Ed stiffened even as he leaned in to kiss her, trying to sense whether Patrick recognized her in her jeans and a sweater, a gold cross at her clavicle—a far cry from the skirt and heels he'd picked her up in, though the outfit hadn't even been that trashy, really. Maybe he'd have believed she was going to a club or to dinner if it hadn't been a Tuesday night—and if they hadn't been doing a prostitution sting two streets over. If she'd just denied it, given him some other excuse for why she was strolling down a known hooker hangout in the middle of the night, he'd never have picked her up at all. But she hadn't denied it, not for a moment. Hadn't really said anything... until later.

He held out the bag. "Oh, so...I got you something."

She peered inside, one eyebrow raised, the corner of her mouth twitching. But when she met his gaze again, she was laughing outright. "You didn't have to, Ed. My dad just says things—"

"I hope you like it." Did she hate this one just as much? But—good news—she was already sliding out of that yellow monstrosity and shrugging into the new purple jacket, her favorite color, though not her favorite shade, something she called "lilac." This coat was purple like a bruise. Was that bad? Or did bruise-purple have a better name he didn't know?

Patrick cleared his throat, and Ed's shoulders tensed again; he'd almost forgotten his partner was there. "Heather, Patrick. Patrick, Heather."

"Hey there," Patrick said, sliding into a seat across from Heather, who flushed but only nodded. She seemed to have lost her voice. "Sounds like you've taken my partner here for one hell of a fast ride."

Ed glanced over as he sat down beside her, and there *was* a twinkle of recognition in Patrick's eye, wasn't there? Or was Ed imagining it? Heather blushed and lowered her gray eyes to her lap, and Ed covered her hand with his. Still so anxious. How had she made it through school? But she'd told him: avoiding bullies and boys by keeping her mouth shut and her head in the books. She'd once joked that if her lips had been sewn together, no one would have even noticed.

"I guess things went a little quick," she said to the table, her voice shaking. *She does know him.* But maybe not—how much of this was anxiety and how much…meant something?

"Hey, I'm not judging." A damn lie. Patrick's face was a mask: still and watchful, the same look as when he caught someone speeding, or jaywalking, or slapping their girlfriend around.

The waitress arrived, but Ed scarcely looked at the woman as he ordered—though he remembered to ask for water with lemon, just to make Heather's lip twitch up. Patrick was on his third marriage. He had no room to judge. *What am I even worried about?* Not like Patrick was going to walk into the chief's office and tattle on Ed with blow right there under his nostrils.

After the waitress left, Heather caught Ed's eye—*Can we leave now?* Patrick didn't seem to notice because he said, "So what're ye doing tonight while I drag your fiancé around in the comin' storm?"

Heather shrugged and kept her gaze on the table in front of them. Donald had told him that when she was a kid, she ran from people who said hello to her. Weird that she thought she'd be okay out there on the street even once— shit, had it really only been once? He should have asked more questions up front, at least asked her why she did it, but it was too late to spring it on her now. If he really cared, he should have asked months ago.

Patrick narrowed his eyes at her, then at Ed, and Ed's lungs seized—*this is it*—but Heather cleared her throat, and Patrick's expression softened.

"Just running some errands for my dad," she said. "Then, I have a meeting."

A meeting. She was always trying to find good deals on wedding favors and cake and even napkins, though they were just having a party for the other shelter volunteers and the church folks—for her father, really, more than them. Ed would've been happy to head over to the courthouse in his uniform. Would she make him wear a tux?

"Tell your dad I said hi," Ed said. Ed glanced down at her boots, her tiny feet, one heel hooked around her chair leg. Bouncing. Still nervous. He touched her arm, but she didn't respond. Had she stopped breathing?

"Heather?"

She finally turned her gaze back to him. "I love the coat."

"Oh…good." But she'd have said that even if she hated it. He gestured to the waitress. "Can I get some more lemon for my water?"

This time, Heather didn't smile.

## 4

---

THE EVENING PASSED slow as molasses, tagging broken taillights, pulling over speeders, answering "suspicious character" calls over people just walking home from their jobs—apparently, everyone looked suspicious in a parka.

At nine thirty, the radio squawked over the incessant patter of the Irishman's fingers on the steering wheel, and the *thunk, thunk, thunk* of wipers against the icy snow. "Ten-thirty-eight, black Ford truck, corner of Mack and Emmerson."

Ed straightened in the seat, squinting through the night. Ahead lay a party store, a gas station, a fast-food restaurant—everything misty behind the screen of falling snow. Mack and Emmerson. Three blocks from where he'd met Heather and right across from the high school in front of a park that had become, in recent days, a hangout for dope dealers. Ed watched Patrick's face in the glare of the streetlamps. His partner'd barely said three words since lunch, but the street around them—so close to the known prostitution zone—was practically whispering in Ed's ears: *Ask him, ask him.* "You sure you've never met Heather before?" The moment the words left his lips, he wished he could take them back. Patrick was no fool.

Patrick kept his eyes on the windshield, but his jaw tightened, and his fingers tensed on the steering wheel. "Should I have?"

*I should just tell him about Heather. Get it out in the open.*

*No, that would be stupid.*

"Nah, but you kinda looked like you recognized her." And she had seemed nervous around Patrick—extra nervous. Or was that his imagination?

Patrick sniffed, hard, then paused for far too long. "I might have seen her around the church," he said. "She go to St. Ignatius?"

St. Ignatius. Donald's church, Heather's church. Patrick was there every Sunday with his current wife, or so he said; Heather usually took her father Saturday nights, but they could have run into each other at some point in the past. Why hadn't he thought of that? *Because you've only gone with her one time—couldn't even name the church on your own.*

He squinted at his partner, and when Patrick didn't turn, Ed looked out the window at the snow cloaking the sidewalks. "Yeah, she does go to St. Ignatius."

"That explains it."

But if Patrick had met Heather there, then why not bring it up at lunch? Wasn't that the ultimate conversation starter? *Hey, we both dig crucifixion and confession, let's be buds!* But... whatever. Ed didn't want to have this discussion anyway, because if Patrick *did* know her from somewhere else...

Patrick turned the corner onto Emmerson, and Ed narrowed his eyes at the schoolyard on their right, the park on their left. The pickup truck sat in the street between those landmarks, its motor rumbling in the otherwise quiet road, tendrils of exhaust belching from the tailpipe and melting the snow beneath it to a shiny puddle. The truck was not black, but a dark blue F-series, scraped to shit, and no license plate—probably stolen or at least unregistered—with a tattered bumper sticker, the front half torn off. The partial words glared at them in the yellowed shine of the streetlamp: *OD* on one line, *FTS* beneath it. Ed squinted through the falling flakes at the back window of the truck. One occupant that he could see, the back of the driver's head a silhouette in their headlights as Patrick slammed the cruiser into park and flashed their red-and-blues. A single squeal of siren cut the night.

The driver's side door flung wide, and Ed put one hand on his gun, the metal a cold but comforting presence as the occupant of the truck emerged with his hands in the air.

*Oh shit.*

Ed's fingers tightened on the gun.

Blood streaked the man's arms, coated his fingers, and surrounded his wrists, soaked the belly of his gray jacket as if someone had stabbed him in the gut. And below the belt… tan khakis, shiny brown shoes, all of it smeared with crimson. The knees of his khakis were a deep maroon, too, as if he'd been kneeling in the mess, an abstract painting done in someone else's fluids. And his hands, his palms spread beside his hips…he was trembling so badly that Ed half thought the gore might come shaking off his frame like water droplets from a dog after a bath. Ed glanced over at the schoolyard as if expecting some book-bagged child to emerge to get caught in the crossfire, but the school remained silent, the lawn empty and white save for a few fresh prints in the powder.

"What the fuck?" Patrick muttered. "Might need an ambulance."

Ed blinked, the snow-shrouded world blurring then vanishing, and suddenly he was back in the Gulf, and his comrade—his best friend—was facedown in the sand, the side of his head missing, brain and bone shining in the desert sun. His heartbeat pounded a frantic rhythm. He blinked again, and the snow returned along with the bloody man standing beside the truck. If this horror show of a man had lost that much blood, no way he'd be standing with that level stare. Should they call for backup or just the ambulance? Hell, maybe both. But Patrick hated calling in for backup unless they were sure they needed it, and how many people did it take to arrest one possibly injured guy?

Ed opened his mouth to say something, he wasn't sure what, but Patrick was already throwing his car door open, feet on the pavement, heading for the dead-eyed man—and moving far too quickly. *Fuck, is Patrick stoned?* Patrick's gun glinted in the streetlights, flakes of snow sticking to the barrel. He stopped near the tailgate. "Hands up! Turn around slowly!" Ed climbed out of the car, too, following his partner's lead, hoping they were doing the right thing. *We should have called it in first. We should have called it in.*

"Turn around!" Patrick yelled again.

The man stared. Why was the guy just standing there? Maybe he was the one who was stoned. Then up went his hands, waist-high, still shaking. Shoulder high. His face remained blank, dull, and dead. Then, he raised one eyebrow as if confused about who they were and why they were there, eyes flicking left, right, behind them, over his own shoulder—

*That can't be good.*

Patrick must have felt the change in the atmosphere as well because he was cocking his weapon, aiming his gun. "Freeze!"

The man remained still, hands in the air. A chunk of something shiny, wet, slid between two fingers and trailed down his palm, then fell to the sludge at his feet with a wet *plip.*

"On the ground, hands behind yer head!" Patrick yelled,

his Irish brogue trickling through more than usual now, turning "behind" into "be-hoy-ned." If Ed hadn't already been listening to his heart on hyperdrive, he would have started panicking.

The bloody man put his hands behind his ears, achingly slow, as if they were watching a movie at quarter speed. Like the man was…stalling. But for what? Unless he *was* waiting—*Oh, fuck*. The guy turned his head ever so slightly toward the open cabin of the pickup…listening. Someone else was in there.

"Careful, Patri—"

*Bang!*

Ed dove for cover as Patrick twisted around like the bullet itself had taken hold of him and sent him spinning. He hit the slushy ground a step in front of the cruiser's bumper with a wet splat.

Another *bang!* split the night, and Ed skirted the car and ducked behind the open driver's side door, raising his weapon. The bloody driver leapt into the truck as a third shot sent chunks of splintered asphalt past Ed's ear. From this angle, he could see the outline of someone else shooting from the passenger seat through the sliding back window, the tiny glint of a metal barrel visible now through the space in the window casing, and there, the glimmer of yellow off the shooter's eyes. But the rest of his face was dark, too dark, and it didn't reflect the light like skin—a black ski mask.

"Patrick!" Ed's voice was swallowed by the grinding of ice and snow under rubber as the truck peeled away. His hammering heart felt as if it were shooting lava through his veins instead of blood. Ed crawled to his partner, the freezing asphalt stinging his knees right through his pants. "Patrick!" The pickup truck squealed around the corner.

The big man rolled over and hauled himself to seated,

grunting. "Man, fuck that guy." Then he vomited into the slush, holding his hand over his bicep.

"I'm calling it in," Ed said, and scrambled to his feet, but Patrick grabbed Ed's uniform jacket with his good hand.

"Just a flesh wound." Patrick pushed himself to his knees, clambering to his feet, and staggered toward the car.

*Loose cannon, they call him. This is why.* The Irish were ballsy.

"You drive," Patrick snapped. *Ye dr-oy-ve.* "The assholes will get away if we wait on an ambulance." Ed couldn't argue that, and far be it from him to deny his partner a chance at justice—besides, he'd seen people walking around with far worse injuries overseas.

"Those fuckers," Pat muttered as they slid into the car. "Ambushed us…like they were waiting for us." He groaned but gestured with his good hand to the front windshield in the direction the truck had disappeared. "Go fuckin' get 'em!"

With Patrick barking into the radio, Ed tore out over the ice, following the tire tracks in the still-falling snow. Down one block, hard right, then down another block, watching the fast fading tire marks. But they lost the prints when they turned onto the main drag where salt had already burned off the freshest layer of white.

"Shite," Patrick muttered. "Freeway is half a mile that way, but he coulda gone arseways on us a ways back." He wiped his neck with the cuff of his jacket. His forehead shone with sweat.

Ed peered up and down the road, but the salted black pavement offered nothing. Somewhere in the distance, sirens approached, probably covering the other side streets. Ed hesitated with his foot poised above the gas pedal, picturing the prints in the snow in front of the school. Were they fresh? Had to be. His hands tightened on the wheel, the swishing of the windshield wipers thrumming in time to his heart.

"Patrick?"

His partner turned to him, eyes tight with pain and fury.

"He sure moved quick for someone who'd lost that much blood."

"Yeah, he didn't move like he was hurt." Patrick shook his head. The streetlamp flashed amber against the mounds of snow. "It could've been shock, but…"

Could've been shock, but it wasn't. That was too much blood for one man to lose and still be conscious, and the stains hadn't spread while they'd been facing off. Ed looked in his rearview at the white road behind them, their tire tracks already half-hidden beneath the falling snow. "Whose blood do you think was on his pants?"

Patrick turned back to the window and groaned.

**5**

———

THE STREET WAS quiet and still now, the streetlamp reflecting the white glare. The snowy spot where Patrick had collapsed was stained pink, but most evidence of their presence—the tire tracks, their footprints—had been softened by the falling snow.

Same as the prints in front of the schoolyard…and those were the ones that concerned him. They'd been made recently, he was sure of it—otherwise, they'd have been covered by the storm.

There was a reason that man had been back here, a reason he'd been covered in blood, a reason that must lie where those tracks ended, out of sight behind the school—a lonely place without much risk of an audience. And if that reason was still alive…

Ed parked in the road and threw the door wide, and then they were off, running across the road toward the school, following the fast-vanishing prints. Three sets of prints, he could see now, and one smaller than the others, a woman or a child, though it was impossible to tell if they were coming or going.

The footprints veered left at the chain-link gate of the school, then around the side of the building, and here they could see pink beneath the newer snowfall. Not good. With that much blood loss, it wasn't likely the third person had walked out of here. They could only hope to find the victim before it was too late.

Ed and Patrick crunched a path beside the prints, their breath hissing from them like the frenetic whispers of spirits. *Please don't let it be a kid.* One crack baby was enough for him, and that kid had *survived.* He'd pulled the kid from a dumpster behind the middle school, shaking, helpless, so far beyond crying, it broke Ed's fucking heart. Even Ed's baby brother, Sammy—dead at six months from some genetic bullshit he couldn't name—had screamed until his heart had finally, mercifully quit.

They rounded the side of the school and slowed, Ed holding his gun in front of him, eyes tracking left and right over the white crusted landscape. The shadows here were deeper, the streetlamps extinguished by the hulking building —even the moon was hidden beneath the storm clouds, the darkness so oppressive and violent it felt as if the snowflakes, stark against the black, were less falling to the earth and more advancing on them. Beside Ed, Patrick switched on his flashlight, but the beam barely penetrated the storm. Flake after flake barreled toward them out of the gloom. The light wavered as Patrick tracked the glow back and forth over the football field. Goalposts stabbed at the sky on either side of the vast expanse of white, but no bleachers—were there supposed to be bleachers? The light trembled again.

"You okay, Pat?"

"Just a scratch, I told ye, ye goat." The light stopped. "Straight back...ye see that?"

Clouds of frost from between their lips split the snow-choked air in front of them; it was hard to see much of anything beyond the whirling white. Ed squinted. No, there *was* something: about a hundred yards away, a sliver of purple visible above the line of snow.

The squeaking crunch of their shoes and Ed's breath both quickened as they headed toward the back of the field. Toward the body—definitely a body, he was sure now, because the mounded shape was right—

Ed froze.

*No.*

He ran, ran harder than he'd ever run in his life, his breathing frantic, lungs screaming, legs burning, cold biting at his cheeks, and he dropped to his knees and plunged his hands into the snow, digging, digging with numb fingers. Her hands emerged first, limp and already half-frozen, and then he was yanking at her new purple coat, pulling the rest of her from beneath the icy white blanket, her sweater, her jeans, her boots.

The rest of the world vanished, sucked into the unforgiving white. Tornadoes of ice pricked his face, trying to slice off tiny pieces of his flesh. And somewhere in that hell, he heard a voice moaning, "No, please, god no, please," over and over and over.

Her lips were blue. Ed's breath left him, his heart spasming in his chest, spasming and not twitching the way Heather's mouth used to before her lips went still and cold—no, this was deep and aching and horrible. Ice clung to her eyelashes, and her face...the bones looked distorted somehow, but he couldn't tell if it was the meager light or if his wavering vision was from the disbelief and sorrow and grief and fury that flickered back and forth in his brain.

"No, please, god, no, please."

The voice...it was him, whimpering through the night. And when he went to feel for a pulse, her skin was slick, so he pulled her closer and put his hand on the back of her head and touched something slimy, not her head, not her hair, not the perfect round shape of her skull when she lay against his shoulder and held him close. He moved his hand to the left, spread his fingers, feeling—*no, my fingers are just numb, that has to be it*—but it was real: an empty place, wide like a cave, and slime, the slime, the slime, and sharp edges...a jagged crown of shattered bone.

Patrick knelt beside him and crossed himself, forehead, chest, shoulder, shoulder. "Jesus, Mary, and... Ed, is that...?"

The man in the street had been covered in Heather's blood—Heather's brain. She had been dead before Patrick was shot, before they'd left the scene after those men in the truck. He'd never had a prayer of saving her.

**6**

———

Ed sat on the edge of his bed, feet on the floor, staring at his pillow. From the end table, her notebook, the book that contained her dreams for their wedding, lay abandoned, missing her touch, missing her voice, missing...her.

*Why? Why?* Wrong place, wrong time? Just some crazy jackass trolling for someone to hurt? Why did it have to be her? The thoughts ran around and around in Ed's brain, but without answers to soothe their frenzied pace, they only jumbled, twisting together until he could scarcely make out the words, let alone the meanings. But even as his thoughts raced, a fuzzy haze settled around him, slowing time to a crawl, its intervals marked only by the ticking of the clock.

Five days of watching the groceries rot. Five nights of staring at the popcorn ceiling, half believing he could still feel her steady breath against his shoulder. Five mornings waking to visions of Heather's bloody skull, Patrick lying on the street, the suspect's crimson arms, the bumper sticker... the sticker...the sticker.

*OD, FTS.* He could think of no business nearby that matched, though he'd spent five days playing with the letters like they were part of some horrible game of hangman. Five days of calling the station to see if they had anything new, but the dress shoes the man had been wearing and the tire marks left by the pickup were too common to identify, and no trucks of that make and model were reported missing in the area the day of Heather's murder. And they couldn't search every truck in the city. *They would if she were high profile.* That chapped his ass. Some days when Ed called, Detective Mueller paused before answering any questions like he couldn't remember Heather's name.

Five days of disappointment. Five days with his chest aching so persistently, he worried his lungs might collapse. Five days of avoiding any and everyone, including Heather's father.

He'd convinced himself that Donald was fine, that Donald didn't need him, that the man was used to being by himself from his lone wolf missions in Nam, but it was an excuse—the truth was, Ed couldn't look into that man's face, didn't want to see the man's tears, see him staring above the bay window at the ornate wooden crucifix that kept watch over his living room, shaking his head, as if he believed Ed was lying to him, that she would, in fact, come home again. The night Ed told him about her death, Donald had put his hands together, locked his eyes on that crucifix, and prayed. He'd still been sitting there when Ed finally left and drove home to his empty house.

Ed touched the pillow now, and for a moment—only a moment—it almost felt warm, as if she'd just left it. He stood. The heady spicy-sweet smell of her, the thick tobacco smell of them, clung to the insides of his nostrils. They'd been happy here. Happy. But...

*It was my first time.*

The pain in his chest intensified, blistering heat expanding into his neck like he had lava in his veins. He hated thinking about it, hated to admit it to himself, but she'd lied to him that night. The coroner's report said she'd had drugs in her gut, lots of them, leading Detective Mueller to decide the motive quickly: OxyContin robbery gone wrong. But you could pick up Oxy on any corner—you didn't have to go somewhere private. And why else would she be out there behind that school, a place known for narcotics and hookers, if not to trade her ass for some downers? He'd been stupid to believe anything she'd told him about her life out on the streets. Just because she'd had no priors didn't mean she was clean.

But he'd known that when he met her—and loved her anyway. Still did.

He headed down the hall and out to the porch, locking the front door behind him, trying not to see the house as she had. *It's perfect for us, Ed. Can I stay?*

*Forever*, he'd said. *Forever.*

And today, he had to say goodbye.

Pulling into Donald's driveway felt like arriving at his own funeral, and it was the death of the life he'd wanted, though he still walked and talked and breathed—but just barely. Donald sat in the living room, wheelchair facing the window, his eyes wide, the crucifix still keeping vigil from the wall above him. Don's hollow cheeks looked more sunken today than usual, and when Ed approached, the man didn't blink. Ed tried to ignore the heavy *thunk, thunk, thunk* of his own heart.

"Donald?"

Roscoe raised his tiny head from Donald's lap, tail wagging excitedly. Heather's father did not answer. *Oh fuck, he's dead.* But then Donald turned, slowly, his face wrinkling as he frowned.

Ed let the air escape his lungs. "Holy shit, I thought you were…you know."

"If only. I have less than a year, they tell me, but I'm not going out today."

*I thought maybe you got tired of living.* But the man's heart was clearly stronger than even Don wanted, and no matter how tired he was, fear of Hell would keep Donald from taking his own life. Heather's father wouldn't miss a moment of suffering.

Donald squinted at the end table, where a square box of glass held a medal and a picture of a much younger man with his sniper rifle, the entire thing obscured by a film of dust. "You know the best thing about that medal, Ed? Every one of those missions, I aimed, I killed, but if I fucked up, the only one who would have died was me. I didn't have to care about anything else—anyone else." He drew his watery gaze to Ed's. "I came home, numb. I'd give anything to feel that now."

"Have you eaten, Donald?"

"Have you?"

*Fair enough.* "Let's get this over with."

<hr>

ED DIDN'T REMEMBER DRIVING, didn't recall pulling up to the church, but there he was, at this brick and stone building that was supposed to be a haven for all those poor wayward souls who still thought they had a chance. Snow spattered the stained glass windows. Lights flickered from behind the glass and reflected off the powder-caked ledge, creating an abstract watercolor that looked too much like the snow behind the school—new snow soaked in Heather's blood.

Ed turned away. These long stone steps would never welcome her in her white dress, the stained glass figures would never see him waiting at the pulpit with Father Norman in his robes for the Catholic ceremony Heather's father would have loved. Ed would never see the light from the hundred candles on the long, low counter in the back of the nave, shine on her skin, nor watch her stride beneath the life-sized angel statue there, its arms raised as if blessing their union. *Forever.*

Donald's wheelchair was a death rattle against the gleaming wooden floors in the entry. Ed stopped short just inside the door, staring off to his right at the alcove behind the confessional booth—Patrick was in the corner, speaking to another man, this one bald and wearing the sleek black coat and black gloves of an assassin: the chief. Ed's hands tightened on the wheelchair handles as Patrick nodded toward them, and the chief turned his beady brown eyes in Ed's direction.

*Nope, not right now, no.* Why did people think they could just show up anywhere they damn well pleased? In this place, in these agonizing, vulnerable moments…it felt like they were watching him shower. Ed showed them his back and continued up the aisle, ignoring the approaching *clap, clap* of his boss's footsteps against the wood and the heavier *thud, thud, thud* of Patrick's rubber soles.

*What the fuck do they want?*

Ed reached the front of the aisle, half a dozen steps from the altar.

"Let me sit here a moment," Donald said, so quietly Ed wouldn't have heard him if not for the echo against the pulpit. The man crossed his fingers in his lap and bowed his head, muttering under his breath, praying to the sculpture above them: a man wearing a crown of thorns, stakes driven through his hands and feet, the terror in that carved face a monument to humanity's wickedness. And that wickedness, the evil lurking around every street corner in this fucking city—no one escaped it. No one.

Ed stepped back from Donald's wheelchair, and as he stared at the cruel slice in the statue's side, wrists dripping blood from wounds no one would bother to tend, the depravity on that crucifix snuffed out Heather's face and replaced his bride with a picture he cared less about. A body he cared less about. His heart slowed.

"How you holding up, Ed?"

*Ed.* In that one word, his own name, he could feel Heather's breath on his neck, could smell her gardenia-infused skin in his nostrils like she was standing right beside him. "As well as can be expected." He kept his eyes on the cross above them, the painted blood, the crown of thorns. "Why are you here?"

"I…" Patrick sniffed hard, irritated. "I just wanted to offer my condolences." His voice rose with each syllable as if he were hurt by Ed's words, but he wasn't fucking hurt, Ed knew he wasn't. He could have paid his respects with a card, or flowers, or whatever the hell people did. Instead, he'd brought their goddamn *boss* to the church, knowing Ed was picking up Heather's ashes. He shouldn't have told Patrick where he'd be. Ed squinted up at the crucifix again, and through his fury-steeped gaze, the statue appeared to be crying tears of blood.

The chief coughed from somewhere behind Patrick, a chesty growl. "I also wanted to make sure you knew you were excused from duty. I called you in the other day to discuss your bereavement leave, but you never showed."

They really had to do this now? Ed dropped his gaze from the cross to meet his boss's glassy stare. "I don't need time off." The chief was a dick for even coming here, especially when all he did at the station was bitch everyone out—blustering like he was trying to make up for a tiny shriveled pecker.

"If you feel you can get right back on the force, more power to you. But some need to take time off to heal." The chief's gaze hardened. "Just know that leave is available, as is counseling—"

"I don't need any—"

"—and let Detective Mueller do his job. I heard you called him a dozen times already. Leave him alone and return my calls instead."

Mueller. The detective assigned to Heather's case. So that's what this was about—the chief had come to the fucking *church* to make sure Ed stayed out of the investigation. "Mueller needed my statement," he snapped.

"He had your statement already, Petrosky."

"Fine." Ed bristled, hands clenched. "Now, if you don't mind…" He turned away. Above them, Jesus sobbed silent wooden tears. *Forever*, he'd said. *Forever.*

*Click, click, click,* the sound of shoes on wood, shoes fancier than the chief's. Ed shifted his gaze to see the priest sidling down the pew, his white robe shhing around his legs. *Thank god, no pun intended.* If he'd said that aloud, Heather would have laughed. Grief electrified the ache in his chest. He cleared his throat as if to clear that pain as well, but it remained hot and stinging. Behind him came the scuffle of his colleagues backing off a step. They were cops, but they were in Father Norman's house now.

"Edward," Father Norman said, voice low and soft. "I am so sorry for your loss." The footsteps behind Ed retreated still farther, and as Ed stepped up and took the handles of the wheelchair again, Norman leaned in closer to his ear. "Do you desire their company, my son? They've been waiting for over an hour, and if you'd invited them, they surely would have come to meet you nearer our appointment instead of…lurking."

Perceptive. Father Norman put his hand on Ed's shoulder, and Ed relaxed his grip on Donald's chair. "No, I didn't invite them."

The priest nodded to the men at Ed's back—"I'll be with you shortly, Mr. O'Malley"—then gestured to the hall behind the pulpit off to the right side of the church. Ed glanced back at Patrick, a man who came here on Sundays but didn't remember meeting Heather, a man who had…what? Two kids with his current wife? He never talked about them, never talked about anything personal—they didn't really know each other, did they? Patrick remained in the middle of the aisle, arms at his sides. Standing his ground like he owned the place. This church and everything in it belonged to men like Patrick O'Malley more than it did to men like him.

"Please…" Father Norman gestured again to the hall near the front of the church and walked in that direction, passing beneath the bleeding wooden Jesus. Ed grabbed the handles of the wheelchair once more and left his partner and his boss standing in the aisle watching after them.

The hallway was warmer than the nave, the stark white walls bringing Ed's vision of Heather in her wedding dress roaring back to him so violently he almost stopped walking, leaving Donald stranded in the middle of the hall. But he forced himself to go on, past an office, then through a scarred pine door that bore a simple golden cross, a lower-case *t* without a human form suffering upon it. Despite the elaborate stained glass, Father Norman lived humbly, as he preached others should; the desk was old plywood, the chairs worn as if purchased in a rummage sale. Norman grabbed a vase—*no, an urn*, her *urn*—from his desktop. Purple, her favorite, though she'd have said "indigo," or "violet," or some name that made it sound better. Nicer. Whatever color it was, the purpose was the same because they'd reduced her to ash like their dreams, poured her in a jar so they could put her on Donald's mantel. Not Ed's—the last he'd ever see of her would be her snow-covered corpse.

Father Norman placed the urn in Donald's lap and laid his hand on the old man's quaking shoulder. "It is my duty to ease suffering," he said, tears in his eyes as he raised his gaze to Ed's. "Yet here...I know words are not enough. Heather will be missed dearly by all of us. The other volunteers loved her."

The other volunteers...maybe they should have had a service. But Heather had only ever mentioned some woman named Gene, and for a moment, Ed couldn't recall if Gene worked in the church or at the shelter where Heather volunteered...no, it was the shelter because she used to call with Heather's schedule. But a service wouldn't ease anyone's suffering. There was nothing to be done, nothing that would bring Heather back.

"She always found such comfort here, in the church," Donald said, his voice tight. But that wasn't true, was it? What had she said? *I think my dad is afraid of what might happen to people who don't believe—so I tell him I do. It's one small comfort I can give him.* Though whether Heather had lied to him or to her father, no one would ever know.

"You're sure you don't want a ceremony?" the priest was saying, lips turned down at the edges. Father Norman hadn't liked the cremation thing—some Catholic superstition, those guys liked their caskets and graves—but Donald was pragmatic. And Ed never wanted to see Heather's shattered skull again, even if they did hide it with makeup and wigs and hats and lace. You could hide anything under lace, but that didn't mean it was gone.

Donald shook his head, and Ed looked down at the purple urn shining in the man's lap—definitely purple like a bruise, like her new coat, and now, Ed would never know a better name for that color. And Heather would have hated a room full of folks sitting there talking about her. She didn't even like speaking to them in life.

*In school, they could have sewn my mouth shut, and no one would have noticed.* And that twitchy little smile. That smile.

Donald reached into his shirt pocket and produced an envelope with shaking fingers. Father Norman took it, peeked, and cocked his head. "Donald, the urn, the cremation…everything has already been paid for."

"For the sake of the soul—tithings keep us clean, Father. I intend to carry on Heather's work here, even if I no longer have the legs to volunteer myself. And we both know I'm not long for this earth. I have no use for it."

Norman's face crumpled, but then he threw his shoulders back and sniffed once, hard, as if trying to suppress his emotions. "Do not hesitate to let the church share your burden,"—he met Ed's eyes—"either of you. Please consider joining us for dinner Thursday night as well."

Thursday night. Fucking Thanksgiving. He'd have to call his mother and tell her that he wasn't coming. He should probably tell her about Heather's death, too, but the thought of ever having to say it out loud again made him feel like puking.

"We'll be staying home, Father," Donald answered for them both. "I'd rather deal with this alone."

*Agreed, old man.*

Father Norman's eyes were locked on Donald now, but the man kept his gaze on the urn in his lap.

"If there is anything, *anything* at all I can do, please let me know."

But the sudden aching void that had brought them to the church was not a hole that any man could fill. Nor, Ed realized, could Heather's God.

## 7

OVER THE NEXT WEEK, Ed's anger simmered, then boiled over, obscuring the world around him in a hot, aching haze. He'd experienced these dark episodes when he was younger too: When his brother Sammy died. When his girlfriend broke up with him, but she'd been a bitch anyway, with her bread-hoarding and homeless-shaming bullshit. The depression had also crept up when his father told him they weren't able to pay for college, so don't even bother—not like Ed could have gotten a scholarship with straight Cs. And again that day in the desert, his best friend beside him, talking, laughing, then *bam!* a sniper's bullet and half of Joey's head had been reduced to red mist.

But this was a different darkness. Heather's face, Heather's voice, the smell of her hair, their dreams of marriage, of children, whirled inside a soul-sucking hole in his chest, the pain dragging him deeper into himself, half a step from implosion. The only thing that kept him from surrendering to grief was the rage, white and hot, that yanked him from the depths so violently, some days he feared he'd snap the thread tethering him to sanity. Nothing was the same—he wasn't the same. And he had no way to tell how he'd feel from one moment to the next. Three months ago, he had run four miles with the fucking flu, and today, he'd only gotten out of bed for work. Even now, as the icy roads whizzed by the cruiser under a dull gray sky that matched his mood, a piece of him was still in that bed, staring at the popcorn ceiling. Exhausted. Pining. Hurting.

"You sure ye aren't going to take time off, Ed?" Patrick had asked the same when they passed the church this morning, the place where he'd blindsided Ed the week before. *Four-leaf-clover-humping asshole.*

"If you can work with a hole in your shoulder, I can sure as shit make it too." *With a hole in my goddamn heart.*

"Yeah, but, Ed—"

"Call me Petrosky. It's more professional."

Patrick glanced at him, his thick eyebrows raised, but Ed —*Petrosky*—kept his face placid. He'd decided on the way back from the church with Heather's urn that he never again wanted to hear his name out loud. He didn't want to recall the way Heather had whispered in the night—*Ed, come here*— or her laughing and slapping his arm after he'd said something ridiculous. *Oh, Ed, you're so silly.* Given enough time, he could make those memories vanish, he'd done it before…if only people would stop reminding him.

Patrick opened his mouth like he wanted to ask something else, and Petrosky willed him to, dared him to, because he craved a little—a lot—of trouble, but the squawking radio cut into his thoughts. Neighbor dispute over a dog, of all the fucking things. At the scene, Petrosky half listened to the bitching of the middle-aged muumuu-in-the-snow hag, who clearly just wanted to screw with someone, then followed Patrick to the neighbor's and watched him issue a ticket for violation of a noise ordinance. A fucking noise ordinance. The twenty-something black man who answered the door pursed his lips but took the slip with a nod, and the tail-wagging pit bull at his heel didn't bark at them once. At least that man had a dog to make the nights less…empty.

*I should visit Donald*, he thought as he climbed back into the cruiser. The man had just lost his daughter, and Donald's bi-weekly visit from the nurse surely wasn't support enough.

Gooseflesh rose between his shoulder blades; Patrick was watching him. Instead of turning his partner's way, Petrosky settled for glaring at the snowdrifts.

"Ed…er, Petrosky?"

Petrosky…yes, that was better. He turned. Patrick's brows were furrowed. "Why didn't you tell me she was a—"

"A what?" Rage boiled in Petrosky's chest. A druggie? A whore? Which Heather did Patrick know about? *Like I needed to tell you, you fucker—you knew from the second you saw her.* And in that moment, there in the car, he'd never been so sure of anything as he was that Patrick had recognized Heather, that he'd known about the prostitution when they met in the diner, the day she died. Probably knew about the OxyContin too. And no one had bothered to fucking tell *him*.

Patrick shook his head. "Never mind, I just—"

The radio squawked again—domestic violence incident—saving Patrick from whatever dumb-shit thing was about to come out of his mouth. But Patrick hadn't said anything wrong, Petrosky realized as his breathing evened, just wanted to know why he'd been kept in the dark. Petrosky had wondered the same himself. Why had it been so easy for her to keep things from him? He should have noticed…something.

He locked his eyes on the snowy landscape as Patrick rolled to a stop at the curb for their next call, decent neighborhood, one of the better ones, anyway. Like the ones he and Heather had often talked about moving to. A maroon lamp lay shattered on the front lawn of the brick colonial, a few reddish shards embedded in the snow of the porch railing like specks of dried blood.

A tall blond man answered the door—one of those entitled prep school jocks Petrosky had seen growing up, whistling at girls they felt certain belonged to them, their pockets fat with daddy's money. And here this cocky bastard was, trying to tell them she'd hit him first. But his knuckles were bloodied, and behind him in the living room, Petrosky could make out a woman sitting on the floor by the La-Z-Boy, legs tucked underneath her, arms wrapped around her thin, nightgowned frame. Her left ear was a mess of stringy hair and congealing blood. How close had this girl come to losing half her skull? Petrosky glanced down at the man's feet —wingtips. Maybe he'd killed Heather too.

*Fucking stupid.*

Patrick pushed past the man into the house, barking into his radio for an ambulance. The woman was shaking her head, eyes wide, staring up at the blond jock in the doorway. A trickle of red dripped from her chin to her chest.

The man put his hands up in a *whoa boy* gesture. "Come on, fellows, I'm a businessman, not a criminal." The smarmy words ran off his tongue like piss down a greasy window, and Petrosky tensed with the desire to strangle him. This man was everything that was wrong with the world—men who took what they wanted without caring who they hurt.

"My god, you're right." Before the guy could smile, Petrosky grabbed his hand and twisted the man's arms behind him, ringing his wrists with steel. "We must have missed the memo where beating your wife suddenly became legal."

"I can pay you," the man said, voice higher, more frantic now. "I don't need another charge on my record."

Petrosky yanked on the man's arm, the bastard stumbling down the steps, then strode over the grass. The wail of an ambulance sounded faintly in the distance. "Well, you're going to get another charge, dickhead, and you're lucky I don't let that girl's father have five minutes alone with you." Petrosky flung him against the car hard enough that the man grunted and lost his footing on the ice, but he reclaimed his balance. Of course he did. Those fuckers always landed on their feet, while the rest of the world collapsed around them.

"Watch your head." He shoved the man forward into the car, and the guy's temple caught on the corner of the door with a *thunk*.

"Hey! Aw, shit, am I bleeding?"

"I told you to watch your fucking head." Petrosky grabbed the door and said, "Now move your feet unless you think your shins will win against metal."

Patrick approached as Petrosky slammed the door, wishing the guy's head were stuck in it. His partner's arm was tucked against his side—still stiff. Was he in pain?

Frosty air bit at Petrosky's nose, fresh and cold and stinging. The blond man in the car said something through the closed window, and Petrosky raised his hand and punched the glass, just hard enough to make the man reel backward in the seat. His knuckles throbbed from the impact. Worth it.

"You better relax." Patrick raised a hand to clap his shoulder, but he must have seen something in Petrosky's face because he lowered his arm and glanced at the man in the car. "Many a time a man's mouth broke his nose."

Petrosky inhaled once more, deeper this time, letting the icicles of frosty air stab straight through his brain. "A man's mouth broke his nose, huh? You think he's going to sneak out of his cuffs and hit me? Is he a fucking magician?"

"Didn't the chief tell you to talk to someone? One of them..." Patrick waggled his fingertips in the air on either side of his head.

"Why see a shrink when I can talk to your sorry Irish ass

for free." But maybe he should see a shrink—before he ended up killing some asshole who didn't know how good he had it, who'd rather beat his wife than love her. Petrosky walked around to the passenger side, steadying his breath before Patrick noticed his shaking hands.

## 8

PETROSKY STARED at the bottle of Jack Daniel's for a week, cursing Patrick for bringing it by—he wanted to feel the pain. To remember Heather just a little longer before he put her out of his head for good. "It'll help you sleep," his partner had said. "Take the edge off, at least." Petrosky had scowled at him, but by the end of week two, he'd cracked it open and let the liquor soften his memories and ease him into oblivion. It was almost too easy to give in.

Which he did each night that week until the bottle was empty. When it was gone, he spent three nights watching the shadows paint horrific images on the popcorn ceiling— bloody hands and Heather's disfigured face, the shattered pieces of her skull. By the time the room lightened each morning, Petrosky's sheets were soaked through with sweat.

He picked up another bottle the evening of day four. After that, the dawn became the worst, when images of Heather with half a head roused him like a gruesome alarm clock. He often woke groggily and reaching toward her, his fingers tangled in cold, slick brain matter.

Instead of hitting the liquor in the morning to erase the

sensation—day-drinking was one step from meetings and sponsors and liver disease—Petrosky threw himself into the job. For three weeks following the procurement of Heather's ashes, he ignored any reference to Heather or the case, which probably made the detective super fucking happy, that lazy bastard. He also ignored Christmas, claiming strep throat, much to his mother's chagrin, but there was always next year. Maybe. And as Ash Park eased into January, the smell of gardenias and incense had begun to subside, and the almost-there sound of her voice had faded. Less so, the images of Heather's shattered skull.

Petrosky clamped his cigarette tighter between his teeth, letting the smoke fog the windshield instead of opening the window to the cold. No snow in the forecast today, but the entire world was still covered in a glassy sheen of ice, glittering darkly—one wrong step and you were screwed. Not that it would matter if he broke something. He wasn't jogging anymore, and he never got to chase anyone in this fucking job. What was the point?

But the point would come back one day, he was sure of it. One day, he'd start running again—start living again. Once the pain eased. One day, he'd forget what Heather's blood smelled like, the same way he'd forgotten almost everything about Sammy, save his name and the sound of his cries. And eventually, those would go too. His father never mentioned Sammy's name at all.

The parking lot of the bagel shop was deserted, the salt crunching under his rubber soles as he headed for the front door. He stopped on the walk in front of the window and was sucking down the last few puffs of his cigarette when he heard: "Can you help me?"

Petrosky whirled around. Cheap heels, cheap jacket, ruddy cheeks like she was going into the bakery to get out of the cold. *Can you help me?* The way he'd tried to help

Heather? For a moment, he could almost convince himself she *was* Heather—that he might have the chance to question her, to undo the horrors of the last months. *What were you doing out at night like that? Why couldn't you have been fucking honest with me? I could have helped you, goddammit!* But he hadn't known what she'd been doing, hadn't known about her addiction; she'd kept that from him, and it had cost her her life. His heart throbbed, much too fast—she'd lied, she'd fucking lied, and now she was dead.

"Do I have sucker tattooed on my forehead?" he hissed.

"What? No…" She flushed a deeper maroon. "You don't understand."

No, he didn't, but as he looked at her, his shoulders relaxed. Her earrings were expensive, even if her jacket wasn't, and her briefcase was real leather. She wasn't looking for a sucker. But what did she need from him, then?

"Sorry," he said, more softly. "What is it you want?"

"My name is Linda Davies," she said with a slight tremble that could have been from anxiety or cold. "I knew Heather."

Petrosky squinted at her. Dark hair, like Heather's, and a heart-shaped face and full lips, but her eyes were hazel, gray-green-blue, and her gaze pinged some little needle of recognition in his spine. "I know you."

"You do."

"From the social work office." They'd never met, but he'd seen her over at the precinct on some case or another. The social work building was a tiny madhouse, full of overworked and underpaid do-gooders trying to service the entirety of Ash Park, and it also housed the big-shit shrink's office where cops went after they killed someone or watched their partner die on a snow-covered street. The chief had suggested Petrosky "hop on over" there like he was a fucking kangaroo the day he'd come back to work. But a shrink wasn't what Petrosky had needed—he'd needed to get out on the road, to distract himself, though that wasn't working…yet.

"That's me." Linda smiled. "I helped Heather get services for her father. But our last meeting…she said some odd things. I've been trying to get ahold of you."

He'd unplugged his house phone a full week ago. His mother had been calling with that tight note of worry in her voice, and he was too worn down to even attempt to convince other people that he was okay.

"Did you follow me here?"

"Yes." She squared her shoulders. "But I wouldn't have had to follow you if you'd returned my calls—I must have rung you ten times since Donald gave me your number."

He waited for her to say more, but she leveled her gaze at him instead, and there was something in her eyes, a spark of intelligence, or maybe tenacity—that same tenacity he'd noticed when Heather told him about taking care of her father, about keeping him out of a home. Determination—that was it. He stared back. "I didn't get the messages."

Linda sighed. "Fine, whatever. But I have something you need to hear." Her voice was pressured, rushed—was she in a hurry? Probably. Even the detective wasn't spending more than the bare minimum on Heather's case. "I know this sounds crazy, but I think Heather's death… She wasn't just an addict out trying to score dope."

"She was an addict; they found her with drugs in her stomach." Petrosky had been in love, but he wasn't a fool. *Even if I am a sucker.* Grief and rage rose, brightened, then settled again as he said: "What makes you think that she wasn't?"

"She didn't need to go out to get drugs; she could have taken the medication from her father. He isn't managing his pain well, doesn't take as many pills as he should."

But Heather wouldn't have taken Donald's medication—

no way she'd allow him to be in pain just to satisfy herself. Or would she? Addicts did stuff like that in the throes of withdrawal, barely even thought about it. And people built up tolerance to drugs fast—she might have started on Donald's leftover pills but couldn't sustain herself that way. And when the demand exceeded the supply, she'd gone out hooking instead of asking for help. *Hooking.* Like she was a piece of meat hanging from the ceiling. His head throbbed. The night they'd met, she'd said it was her first time…what if that *was* the first time, but she'd kept doing it after they'd met? What if she'd been living in his house and when he was at work, she'd been…she'd been…

*Liar, liar, liar,* and in his head he could see her glassy, stoned irises, see her naked flesh, pants around her ankles, see her bent over with her hands against the brick building, some greasy dealer behind her, thrusting, thrusting, and another man watching, waiting his turn, and her moaning long and low the way she had with Petrosky—maybe she'd faked it with him too. Fire and bile clogged his throat, and the image of her fucking some stranger against the school-house vanished, replaced with Heather the last time he'd seen her: her eyelids crusted with ice, the snow-flecked jelly of her brain matter on his hands.

He cleared his throat, trying to ignore the way Linda cocked her head—concerned. "The detective said her death was drug related." What Detective Mueller had said specifi-cally was, "She was trying to get high as a freakin' kite, and someone smashed her head in with a crowbar and took her shit." The crowbar had been found nearby, no prints. Like most detectives he'd met, Mueller was a dick—hardened, pompous like the world owed him something, as if any of them would end up better than worm food. Though that had been the eighth time Petrosky had called. Sudden pain seared his fingers, and he looked down to see his cigarette butt had burned down to the filter. He tossed the butt into the snow, where it fizzled out with a hiss like an angry snake.

Linda lowered her eyes. "Like I said, the drug thing isn't ringing true to me, and I have some experience in that area, and not just from work." She blushed again. "My uncle was… Listen, that doesn't matter. I see lots of women, Detective—"

"I'm not a detective." Just a flatfoot with a boulder between his shoulder blades. Maybe he'd go back to the military and get his face blown off, go out in a haze of red mist.

"Whatever. I need to tell you this so I can sleep at night." She took a deep breath, and the compassion written on her face made his shoulders relax again, but not his chest—his heart throbbed painfully against his ribs. "I met with her the day she died. At her father's."

Petrosky frowned. At the diner, Heather had said: "I have a meeting." Apparently, it was with Linda, who'd probably been telling Heather to put her father in a home—again. No wonder Heather was anxious at lunch that day.

Linda's voice pulled him out of his head and back to the snowy walk. "She got a page when I was there. I heard it beep, and she tucked it away when she saw me looking, but she was upset—far more nervous than I've ever seen her."

"Donald gave her that pager in case of an emergency." But they hadn't found Heather's pager at the scene or anywhere else, a fact Mueller should have found significant—it took an idiot to discount something like that. And Mueller was no idiot. Petrosky's chest burned. In the military, you followed orders, and you learned to trust your commander and your comrades completely. But here…something was wrong. And out in the sand, you learned to trust your gut, too, or you ended up dead.

"Donald was in his room when I was speaking to her, so clearly someone else has that number," Linda said, dragging him from his thoughts once more. "I'm sure the detective looked into the pager already as a matter of procedure, but it all seems so…like they aren't trying hard enough. And Donald deserves to see his daughter's killer put away before…" She blew her hair out of her face. "Anyway. I just think the detective is wrong about her death being drug related. I think someone lured her out there behind that school on purpose. I think Heather knew the person who killed her too—I think she was in trouble from the moment they paged her. And I needed to tell someone who cared." With a final nod, she turned and headed back over the snowy lot, leaving Petrosky staring after her.

**9**

---

LINDA'S WORDS rang in his head all morning, irritating the edges of his brain. Was she right about this? Had one of the men in the truck—either the bloody man or the ski-masked shooter—lured Heather there on purpose? Chosen her? Chosen to reduce her to pieces, reduce her to a shattered skull, that horrid crown of bone, and the slime, the cold, her eyelashes crusted in snow, and her purple coat... Petrosky tried to push the images from his mind as he drove to the precinct, but the lava in his veins grew hotter with each mile. Who had killed her, and why the hell would they want her dead?

By the time he parked his car in the precinct lot, his heart was beating so furiously that his hands shook. He couldn't go on like this—he'd bitten that poor woman's head off this morning, and all she'd done was...*care*. About Heather. He had to shut it off, the way he had overseas, the way he had in the sand after he'd watched Joey die. Suddenly his nostrils stank of gunpowder and dust.

*The fuck you want to be, boy?*

*Numb, sir.* His own father hadn't shed a tear when Sammy

54

died, hadn't even taken a day off work. That was the way you made it through, the way you made it home from war, and learning how to shut out the world had made his entire stint overseas worth it. Sammy's death had hurt up until then. But not after. And not now. But Heather… He sucked in a breath over clenched teeth.

Petrosky turned the engine off and sat in his car, letting the rapidly cooling air tingle his sinuses, watching the icicles that hung from the precinct roof like knives—opaque cones, water turned deadly, glittering in the sun. He watched the icicles. Just the ice. And by the time Patrick emerged from the building and waved him over, Petrosky's hands no longer shook. He lowered himself into Patrick's squad car, channeling his father in the days after his brother Sammy died, and rebuilt his face in stone.

DETECTIVE MUELLER WAS in the bullpen when Petrosky got off his shift, the man's potbelly pressed against the edge of his desk, his haphazardly buzzed gray-and-black hair spiking from his head. He lifted his jowly face as Petrosky approached.

"Get any leads on the Heather Ainsley homicide?" Almost Heather Petrosky. Almost.

The man grimaced at Petrosky's badge like his visitor didn't belong there—because he didn't. "Didn't the chief tell you to stay off this case?"

"Fuck the chief."

Mueller's eyes widened. He crossed his beefy arms.

"What about the gun, at least? Come on, man, give me a break."

Mueller's jaw tightened, and for a moment, Petrosky thought the detective was going to tell him to fuck off, but the man lowered his arms and sighed. "Don't have much. Everything was snow, slush, no way to get good footprints. And the bullet from your partner's shoulder didn't help—.38 special, but without a gun to compare it to..." Mueller turned back to his desk, back to the file in front of him—a case that obviously mattered more than Heather's. "Seriously, though, the chief told you to leave it be. Let's pretend you were never here."

Petrosky bristled. "I'm not going away. Someone should care, even if she was a druggie whore." He spat the words. God help him if he ever ended up like one of these hardened bastards—what a miserable fucking existence.

Mueller whirled back with his eyebrows raised. "What are you talking about? No one said anything about her being a whore. She wasn't dressed like one, and she didn't have signs of vaginal trauma, no evidence of recent intercourse either—no fluids."

No fluids? Heather hadn't been hooking? He'd been so ready to believe it, so ready to believe the worst of her. Something warm shivered down Petrosky's spine.

"Plus, we talked to every hooker who stakes claim on that street, trying to find a witness." Mueller drew his shoulders back. "None of them knew who she was."

Petrosky stared at the desk. If she'd been out there only for the drugs...was it better to be a druggie than a whore? But she'd never denied it, she might as well have told him she was a— "Maybe Heather just hadn't met the women you asked," he said slowly.

Mueller snorted. "Trust me—streetwalkers pay attention to new meat."

Petrosky's chest tightened, but a slow, warm heaviness had settled in his belly. Not a whore, not that night. Just there for the drugs; the area was known for having dealers, but they hung out in the open, where they could sell. He'd assumed Heather went behind the school to perform some sexual act for the pills, but if she hadn't...then what was she doing back there? Maybe Linda was right—someone asked her to meet them. "What about the pager? Did you look into who called her?"

"No pager on her person, but yes, we checked out the records. The only page that night was from a pay phone over on Breveport. We assumed it was her dealer."

Breveport, by the homeless shelter. Almost the same place Petrosky had arrested her the night they'd met.

Mueller met Petrosky's eyes. "Listen, I did my best here, okay? But there was nothing to go on. She was stoned out of her mind, even if she did try to puke it up when she realized she might OD."

*Puke it up?* "You never mentioned that."

"I wasn't sure until forensics finished with all the samples out there—you saw it, that place was a mess." Mueller filled him in: Heather'd had intact pills in her stomach, which he knew, but they'd found more intact pills and her half-digested dinner hidden beneath the snow in front of her, and injuries on her knees from kneeling. "She also had abrasions in the back of her upper esophagus, and tissue under her fingernails. She rammed her fingers down her throat," Mueller said. "Must have realized she'd taken too much."

"If she threw up before the pills broke down, the drugs wouldn't have hit her yet, not enough to make her think she was OD'ing."

"She still could have sensed something was off—counted pills, seen she'd taken more than her body could tolerate."

Or...someone had been trying to hurt her. *I think Heather's death... She wasn't just an addict out trying to score dope.* "Maybe she never wanted to take them at all."

"Didn't want to..." Mueller scoffed. "I know she was your girl, but man—"

"If she was on her knees, incapacitated, why would someone smash her head in? Even if she wasn't heaving, there were two other people with her, two killers on one vulnerable woman. They didn't need to hurt her to rob her." Heather wouldn't have resisted during a robbery attempt— she could barely speak to strangers, let alone argue with them. And the assailants had to know neither hookers nor druggies were likely to call the cops if they got robbed of their illegal substances.

"Why kill her?" Mueller said, incredulous. "For fun? These psychos are fucked up, half do it for the thrill. Same reason they broke her ribs. ME says it looked like they stomped on her chest after the fact too." He winced. "Sorry."

*Stomped her*. Jesus Christ. Bile rose in his throat, but he swallowed it back and said, "Clearly, they intended to kill her —that could have been the main objective." Linda certainly seemed to believe it. "What if they made her take the pills to kill her, and when she stuck her fingers down her throat, they came back to finish the job?" His head felt as if it were stuffed with cotton.

"Right. Some other addicts gave her pills instead of taking them, smashed her head in, searched her pockets for more drugs, then wandered off to wait for the cops." He shook his head. "Robbery was the main objective whether the death was purposeful or accidental. The perp you saw was fucking *high* off whatever they stole from her—even when he saw you and Patrick, he just stood there."

But the guy in the pickup cab had sure aimed with impressive precision. Linda's voice rang in his head again: *The detective is wrong about her death being drug related. I think someone lured her out there behind that school on purpose. I think Heather knew the person who killed her too—I think she was in trouble from the moment they paged her.*

Heather hadn't been hooking like Petrosky thought. And

if there was a nugget of truth in Linda's words, if Heather wasn't a druggie either…then maybe Petrosky *had* known her. Or enough of her. Enough that what they'd had together was real. And these bastards had taken her from him, the stoned bloody man and his trigger-happy friend.

The fuckers were going down.

## 10

————

*I SHOULDN'T HAVE COME HERE. If Donald knows anything, he would have told Linda.*

Petrosky kept his eyes on the wooden mantel, where Heather's urn stared back at him—purple, but not like a bruise. Purple like the lips of a dead woman. And though just seeing the urn twisted his guts in a knot, Petrosky would rather gaze at it than look at what Heather's father had been reduced to.

The man's cheeks were shrunken, hollow, the dark beneath his eyes so pronounced it looked like he'd been punched. "You'll need to take Roscoe soon." Donald's voice trembled, probably as much from disease as from sorrow. "I don't think I can care for him any longer. Not without Heather."

Petrosky dragged his gaze from the mantel, past the brick fireplace, past the wooden paneling to the pinscher seated in Donald's lap. The little dog's head was so tiny a man could crush it in his fist. His heart seized. Roscoe's ears perked up, his tail thumping against Donald's leg, but his eyes looked sad, droopy. Maybe the pup missed Heather too.

"I'll try to find him a good home." Petrosky stared down at Donald, then at Roscoe, his little puppy eyes closed once more. How sad would Roscoe be if Petrosky never came home from work? The next bullet from a truck window might not miss. "I'm not around enough to take care of him." He was home as little as possible now; he couldn't bear feeling that Heather might come strolling through the door with groceries for dinner or a movie from the rental place. Illogical, yes, but it hurt to have that hope crushed every night. And even thinking of moving out felt like he was abandoning her.

Donald sniffed, his eyes on the dog. "I'll ask one of the fellas at bingo tonight."

Bingo. Donald's one big excursion every week—seemed he was trying to avoid sitting at home alone too.

"That's a good idea." The silence stretched as Donald stared out the window…no, stared *above* the window. At the crucifix. Petrosky suddenly wished for sandpaper, wanted to reduce those carved wounds to smooth wooden flesh.

Donald moved his hand to the top of the dog's spine and stroked Roscoe, fingers trembling, back and forth, back and forth. On the couch, a paper bag sat against one brown plaid cushion; the salad Petrosky had picked up from a fast-food joint the day they'd gone to the church to collect what was left of Heather. One side of the white paper was speckled with dark fuzz. Soon the mold would be on the cushions, spreading like a virus until it took over everything in this house, obscuring the sparse walls, choking the one lone houseplant on the bay windowsill, snuffing out the little yippy dog in a blanket of suffocating blackness.

Donald couldn't stay here without help, even if someone bought groceries and came in to clean. Heather had been wrong about him being self-sufficient. This place would fall apart without her.

But that wasn't why Petrosky was here tonight. Linda's words—*The detective was wrong about it being drug related. I think she knew the person who killed her*—echoed in his ears. If there was any chance she hadn't gone to meet a dealer; if she'd been killed for any other reason…he needed to get to the bottom of it. And Donald might know more than he thought he did.

Donald wiped a hand over his forehead and grimaced.

"How's your pain, Donald?"

"Okay."

"I talked to Linda, the worker who comes by here sometimes. Sounds like your meds aren't working as well as they could be."

"Slaves to pills, to the bottle…the users will be cast down. I have my faith. I don't need drugs."

Donald apparently thought addicts went straight to the fiery pits of Hell. Had anyone told him about the drugs in Heather's system? "Donald…are you telling me you don't take your pain pills at all?"

"Jesus suffered for us." His eyes went glassy. "We owe him that, too—our suffering."

But Petrosky was barely listening. Donald hadn't been taking his pills, but Heather filled those prescriptions for him every week. He heard Linda's voice again: *She wasn't just an addict out trying to score dope.* But Mueller could be on to something, too, if Heather had stolen the pills from her father to sell them. A robbery gone wrong.

"Did Heather ever take your pills, Donald?"

"Absolutely not." His head snapped in Petrosky's direction, jaw muscles tight. "Heather was a good girl," he whispered, voice lower. "A good, good girl."

Good was irrelevant. Good people did bad things all the time. "Donald, the scene where she died—"

He put up one shaking hand, and Roscoe raised his head,

staring at Petrosky, agitated too. "Ed, I'll tell you the same thing I told that detective—I don't want to know. No man wants to hear about their child's last horrible hours…" He turned his face away.

But what man could live knowing their child's killer was still out there? If Petrosky had a daughter, he'd do everything in his power to find the bastard who'd hurt her. *Fuck it.* If Donald wouldn't do this for his daughter, Petrosky would do it for his bride—and Donald had lived with her, he had to know something. "Heather had drugs in her stomach," Petrosky said before he could change his mind. "The police think she was killed for them, that she was an addict."

Donald whirled back to Petrosky. His eyes flashed fire. "You can't possibly believe—"

"I don't." *At least I don't think I do.* "But I want to know why she died—I need to know, to have an explanation, or every time I close my eyes, I have to see her as she was when I found her. I can't get that picture out of my head."

Donald turned away again, staring at the cross, perhaps wondering which pain was worse—nails through your hands, or invisible nails through your heart. "Maybe she ran into some bad folks at that shelter," he said slowly. "I told her volunteering there was a bad idea. But Heather…she wanted to help people." His lip trembled. *A good, good girl.*

But Mueller had already interviewed the shelter workers because of the page Heather had received from the pay phone out front. Only a few of them ever interacted with her, and the only person Heather had talked about was Gene, who used to call with her schedule. "Have you heard anything from Heather's friend Gene?" he asked. "If she knows something about Heather, anything at all…"

"I don't think he knows much."

*He?* "Wait, Gene is a guy?"

Donald nodded. "Used to call here all the time, had a

thing for her, but he wasn't her type." He shook his head and grimaced, but something twinkled in Donald's eyes, a hint of…righteousness. "Didn't go to church at all, just worked at the shelter. Damn heathens. Father Norman should know better than that."

Heathens. *I wonder how pissed he was when Heather started dating me.* "Did you ever meet Gene?"

"Came by here a few times. Geeky fella, the kind you wouldn't look twice at on the street." Donald sniffed hard, shrugged.

But the ones you wouldn't look twice at were sometimes the most dangerous. The tiny black widow. The jock on the football field with his blond hair shining, grinning, perfect… until he took you home and broke your face.

"Someone at work?" Donald was saying. "She never talked about those people, but if someone there didn't like her… I can't imagine that, but…"

Heather didn't work anywhere but the shelter. Just taking care of Donald was a full-time job. "She wasn't working another job, Donald."

"What are you talking about? Of course Heather had a job."

Was the old man going senile? "Where do—"

"Did some bookkeeping."

"For who?"

"Oh, I'm not sure, exactly. Banks and the like."

*What the…?* No, that made zero sense. "Banks have internal bookkeepers, Donald."

"Stop looking at me like that, Ed." He glared. "She's been doing it since she was a kid—since her mother died. If not for her…I just don't know what I would have done." His eyes filled, and he raised one trembling hand to wipe the tears from his cheek. "You can have a look in her room. That's where she kept the files she was working on. I can't get to them with..." He gestured to the chair. "Too tricky to maneuver in there."

Petrosky headed down the hall, Donald's wheelchair squeaking behind him, past the bathroom, then the spare room where an old treadmill hulked in the corner, a remnant of a time long past, back when physical therapy might have meant locomotion. Now, Donald did physical therapy just to avoid atrophy. *Daddy doesn't want to get rid of that treadmill even if he can't use it; he has trouble letting go of things.* Petrosky's rib cage tightened. Someday, someone might find him dead at fifty-five with Heather's notebooks clutched in his fist, his unused running shoes cracked and dusty beneath the bed.

Heather's doorknob seemed abnormally hot in his hand, and he pushed it in with a sound that was less creak and more scream. Donald stopped his wheelchair at the entrance —the doorjamb was a touch too narrow for him to follow.

Heather's desk sat by the back wall, tiny, stark white against the brilliant purplish-pink wallpaper. *Lavender,* she whispered in his ear. No keepsakes, no mess, no pictures. The open closet showed a long, empty top shelf and a row of sundresses, all the out-of-season things she hadn't yet taken to Petrosky's house.

"Bottom drawer, I think," Donald said from behind him. "I saw her throw her files in there once."

Petrosky walked over the shag carpet—baby blue, matted, but clean—and bent, expecting a shriek as he opened the drawer, but it was eerily silent as if someone had oiled the slide. *Huh.* File folders sat stacked inside, all crisp and clean as if she'd just purchased them, none of the creasing his own files had from opening and closing them dozens of times. He picked up the top one and flipped it open. Lined graph paper with rows of numbers on every line top to bottom, arranged in eight columns.

"What are all these?"

Donald shrugged, and Roscoe opened his eyes and glared at Petrosky again for disturbing his nap. "I never was good at math."

This wasn't math—or bookkeeping. There should be labels on the rows, details for each expense or income source, something to explain what the numbers represented. Even the folders themselves weren't labeled with company names or years. He flipped to the next page: Three unlabeled columns of what appeared to be random numbers, one through one hundred. But the next page was blank. So was the one after. Petrosky flipped again, and again—at least twenty more pages, all empty as if she'd purchased a ream of graph paper just to stuff the files, but on the back of one sheet near the end was a small notation, barely visible… because someone had erased it. He held it up to the light: "Big Daddy" in fifteen-year-old-girl bubble letters, inside a tiny heart.

Big Daddy didn't sound like a bookkeeping client or even a boyfriend—Big Daddy sounded like a fucking pimp. And what was with all the papers? Unless…she'd wanted Donald to think she was doing something legitimate. *What the hell is going on here?*

Petrosky tucked the file under his arm. Either these were real numbers from a real bookkeeping job that she'd miraculously gotten when she was fifteen, or she'd faked the folders so her father wouldn't get suspicious about the influx of cash.

Petrosky was betting on the latter.

And if that were true, where *was* her money coming from? No way this wasn't related to her death. Petrosky turned. Donald was watching him from the doorway, brows furrowed, one hand on Roscoe's back, the wheels of his chair just beyond the jamb. Petrosky squinted, noticing a tiny hairline crack that ran along the door molding…and the molding around the jamb seemed thicker than usual. He took a step nearer. Yes, that crack went around the entire door, a tiny line that separated the original molding from the extra layer someone had installed.

"I… Can I help you, Ed?"

Petrosky drew his gaze away—it must have looked like he was staring at the man. "No, nothing to help with." Just something to figure out. Heather had added an extra piece of wood to the existing frame, ensuring Donald couldn't wheel in here to poke around—definitely hiding something. *At least I'm not the only one she lied to.*

"If you want to bring the folders to the living room, I can look with you," Donald said. "It's just hard getting around is all." Petrosky glanced back to see Donald rubbing his thigh with a shaking hand. "It's been difficult to do…most things with Heather gone."

"I'm sure it has." And that wasn't going to get better. Even Petrosky was only doing the bare minimum around his house, and he had two working legs. "Maybe we should start looking into nursing homes, Donald." Petrosky would help him sell the place, but he'd take her files home tonight, look through every sheet until he had an answer.

Donald shook his head. "I can't afford it, not with Heather gone."

The room heated. "You pay as much here, between the mortgage and nursing assistance. Just take the money you'd use for that and roll it into an assisted living place."

"I can't afford this house anymore, either."

But he'd been able to afford it when Heather was here— when she was "bookkeeping." The folder under Petrosky's arm weighed a thousand pounds. "Are you saying that Heather…that your daughter was taking care of the bills?" His voice came out a whisper.

Donald's fingers traced the middle of Roscoe's head,

again, again, again. "I bought this house after her mother died—I couldn't bear to look at the room where Nancy...shot herself. But the money from the sale of the old house ran out quick, and with the medical bills—"

"You're telling me your fifteen-year-old daughter was paying your mortgage?" *He'll be fine. I've been saving since my mom died, just in case.* Petrosky had thought she'd been managing Donald's money for him. He'd missed something major. But so had Donald.

Petrosky headed for the closet, heart pounding in his throat, checking the pockets of her spring jackets, running his fingers over the back wall, searching for secret compartments, lifting the edges of the carpet. Nothing.

"What are you looking for in there, Ed?"

He couldn't answer—the heat in his chest was scorching, burning his vocal cords. *What were you into, Heather?* What was *he* looking for? Evidence of what she was really doing at fifteen since no one would have hired a bookkeeper that young—and no way she was making enough from any legal after-school job. But did he have to look? She'd had a million reasons to deny being a prostitute, and she never had, not once. And what else, what the fuck else could she have been doing so young that would have paid for an entire household?

"Please, Ed, just...stop."

Petrosky swallowed hard. He ran his fingers under the desk—looking for a key? A note?—but came up empty. The other drawers held a lip balm and one lone piece of chewing gum. Dust bunnies fluttered beneath the bed. Fifteen years old. Damn. But Mueller had said that not a single other working girl recognized Heather, so she couldn't have been walking the street every night for a decade. Had she been an escort? A call girl? All she needed was one rich sugar daddy... *Big Daddy.* Was that why she'd called him that?

Mueller's explanation was still a possibility: drugs. She might have been selling, either then or now. He couldn't prove anything, but…no other explanation fit as neatly. Sometimes the right answer was the most obvious. Hooking or drugs—either would have brought in fast cash. Both would have brought in even more.

Donald was watching him. Stupid or blind, it didn't matter—she'd have been better off elsewhere. His heart ratcheted into overdrive as he imagined Heather at fifteen, her eyes wide and tearful—desperate. Doing god knows what to make enough to pay her father's mortgage. *God knows what.* He could imagine the what. He saw her again, pants at her ankles, some strange man behind her, moaning, moaning…

Petrosky grabbed the folder from the desktop and snapped it open in front of Donald's face. The man's jaw dropped. "What's that?"

"What your daughter was working on."

"They're blank."

"She wasn't a bookkeeper—she was a call girl…or a dealer." Had to be. What other explanation was there?

Donald's jaw dropped. "No. No, there is no way—" His fingers stopped on Roscoe's collar, and the dog yipped as if Donald had pinched him. Donald drew his hand away, and Roscoe jumped off the man's lap and skittered down the hallway.

"How could you have had no idea, taking her money, month after month—"

"She said she came by the money honestly, that she was working, and I couldn't… We'd have been on the streets." Donald's nostrils flared, his lower lip trembling. "I'd have lost her to some foster care family who wouldn't have been able to help her, not the way she needed to be helped—to be saved."

"Saved?" *You selfish piece of shit.* Fathers weren't supposed to take advantage of their kids; they were supposed to protect them. "You think you were saving her by forcing her to take care of the bills? God knows what she had to do to—"

"You're wrong!" But the quivering of his lip told Petrosky that Donald had suspected something more illicit than bookkeeping long ago, and the man wasn't fucking stupid. But he'd never done a damn thing to help his daughter.

Donald straightened, and for a moment, the shaking stopped, and his shoulders went ramrod straight as they must have been in his youth before the disease took hold. Then he slumped over again. "All the pain I've ever had… none of it compares to the pain in my heart now, Ed. I pray you'll never have to suffer the loss of a child."

*I won't.* Petrosky would rather be alone forever than risk loving—and losing—again.

"First that detective, then the social worker, and now you…" Donald was muttering now, shaking his head. "Talk to one another and leave me be. Heather's body, Heather's finances…every time it's another knife in my heart."

*Heather's finances. The detective, the social worker, and now you…* Had Linda been here again since they'd spoken? Did she know about Heather's mystery job?

"When was the social worker here?"

Donald paused so long, Petrosky thought the man hadn't heard him. Then: "I thought she must have spoken to you. Isn't that why you're asking about money?" Donald touched his empty ring finger, maybe remembering a time back before he had a wife, before he had a family, before Heather even existed. Back when he'd been numb. Missing those moments for their lack of pain. "She was here last night," Donald said, one step above a whisper. "Now get out."

Last night. Linda was still investigating.

Linda knew something Petrosky didn't.

11

ACCORDING to the receptionist at the social work office, Linda was supposed to get off work at five o'clock, but it was six thirty-five, and she still hadn't emerged from the building. The darkness around Petrosky felt thicker than it had when he'd parked his Grand Am in the back of the lot, beyond the reach of the streetlamps, and more claustrophobic still after the sky blackened to charcoal behind the fresh storm clouds. At six forty-five, the skies opened, dumping heaps of wet snow—sleet to hail and back—onto the lot…and onto his windshield.

What was he doing here? Stalking a woman? *Returning the favor.* She was clearly investigating Heather's case, snooping around Donald like that, but hopefully, she was doing a better job than the asshole detective who'd barely waited for the autopsy before letting Heather's case go cold. Petrosky lit a cigarette and let the smog tighten his lungs and focus his brain. He didn't bother cracking the window, though he did flick the windshield wipers on; the snow had already encased him in a bubble of glittery slush.

At twenty past seven, the glass door opened, reflecting

the jaundiced shine of the streetlights onto the bushes beside the walk. Linda pulled her coat tighter around her as she strode toward the back of the lot, where her Buick LeSabre was parked down the row from Petrosky's car. Looking up her tags would be frowned upon by the brass, but it was a little thing—not like one breach of protocol was a slippery slope to forgoing procedure altogether.

Even if it had made things easier for him.

He turned the wipers off and watched Linda's silhouette through the falling snow, her footsteps clapping against the salted asphalt, and when she was three hundred feet away, he clenched the cigarette between his teeth and climbed out of the car. She froze in the middle of the lot. Watched him with her fists balled at her sides.

"Linda?"

Her muscles were coiled like a gazelle ready to run, but her shoulders relaxed when she recognized him. She marched over. "What are you doing out here? You scared me half to death!"

"Tell me what you know about Heather's case."

"I already told you what—"

"I just came from Donald Ainsley's house," he said, and her eyes narrowed, their breath pluming around them. Snow clung to her lashes—*like Heather's, like Heather's*—and he had to resist the urge to brush it away. Instead, Petrosky inhaled ice into his lungs, letting it mellow his frantic breathing.

"Why were you there, Linda? What do you know?"

She stared for a beat, then: "I found some…inconsistencies in Donald's paperwork." She crossed her arms and shivered. "Before Heather died, I'd offered to find additional resources for her father. She refused, said it was covered." She glanced back at the building as if hoping someone would walk out and save her from this line of questioning, or maybe making sure they were alone—what

Linda was doing wasn't covered in her job description. But no one else came through the doors. The building might have been a mirage, half obscured by the mess still falling from the sky.

"Heather was right: it *was* covered," Linda said. "Donald was getting most of his services through the state, even physical therapy, though he didn't need that anymore. But he did need the home health aides Heather was paying out of pocket for, and last week one of those checks bounced."

"Oh, I get it. You didn't get your money, so you figured you'd chase Donald down for it?"

"I work for the city. I'm not the collections department." Her eyes were fiery like they'd burn through the snowflakes and into his brain, and Petrosky stepped back. "I went out there because, if the checks were bouncing, Donald would need new services through the state, and I had to make sure he was receiving them."

"That and to poke around in Heather's case a little more."

"You of all people should want to find out what really happened! I needed to know the truth after my boyfriend…" She rubbed her arms with her gloved hands and, for a moment, she looked ten years younger, the haze of floating ice haloing her head in the glare of the streetlamp, her hazel eyes reflecting the light like beacons, her cheeks cherub pink with cold. "Listen, can we go somewhere else? I'll tell you everything I can"—she glanced back at the building again—"just not out here. It's fucking freezing."

"Fine. Want to get a drink?" He definitely needed one, and if it would loosen Linda's tongue…

She nodded and headed for his car. "You drive. I'm tired."

Their footsteps were muted against the skin of precipitation on the asphalt, *thup, thup, thup,* mingling with the *tick tickity-tick* of the still-falling ice. Linda stopped at his passenger door, but he continued to the trunk and shoved his key into the lock. The fresh bottle of Jack Daniel's glinted dully.

"Don't need to drive anywhere," he said, slamming the trunk with a *clank*. "I've got the bar with me."

"You want to sit in the—"

"Makes it easy." He was here to get information, not go on a fucking date.

The purr of the engine drowned out the surrounding world, the interior light casting them in a dim glow that bounced off the snow-encrusted windows—like being trapped in a just-shaken snow globe. He cracked the cap and passed her the bottle. She stared for a moment but took it and slugged back a shot, wincing, then passed it back to him.

"So tell me, Ms. Davies, what exactly do you think you know?" The dry air from the heat ducts fried his nostrils as the liquor burned down his gullet.

She averted her eyes, squinting out the windshield into the storm. "The services for Heather's father, the home health aides I mentioned…Heather paid for those with checks from a joint account."

He set the bottle on the console and warmed his numb fingertips over the heating duct. "So? If Heather was paying her father's bills, it makes sense they'd have a joint account."

"Her father wasn't the other name on the account," Linda said. "I called about the bounced check, and they gave me another name: Otis Messinger." She jerked her fingers through her hair, frustrated. "But he isn't listed with the DMV, and the social security number for Messinger that Heather gave the bank was bogus—and I say 'Heather' because no one at the bank saw this Messinger at all, not once in the last ten years since they opened the account."

Petrosky grabbed the bottle again. Heather'd had a bank account with some other man for ten damn years, and try as he might, he could think of no reason for a man to be paying her that kind of cash at fifteen unless he was having her do something illegal. His blood boiled so hot, he was shocked the snow falling around the car didn't melt on contact. He slugged back another shot.

"That isn't all." Linda took the bottle, her jaw hard. "The day after Heather died, the money was gone. Enough for another five years of care for Donald, pulled in a single wire transfer—and Messinger was the only one with access to the funds." She tipped the bottle up, the Jack glowing amber in the snow-dimmed light. "That's why the check bounced."

*He'll be fine. I've been saving since my mom died—just in case.*

Linda yanked her coat tighter, shivering.

Heather'd had money, more than enough for her father to stay in his own place until he died. And someone withdrawing the money the day after her death was far too coincidental. This Otis Messinger...had he killed her for the money? Or maybe he was the man who had been employing her. That Big Daddy thing could have been just a doodle, but...it felt like more.

"I went to visit Donald to see if he knew who Otis Messinger was, to see if Heather had checkbook balance slips, anything that might help me prove something was wrong, but he seemed oblivious. I kept investigating though, and last night I found something at the homeless shelter right up the road, the place Heather's last page came from."

"How do you know where Heather's—"

"I've been working with your department for five years. I have sources too." She sniffed, self-righteous.

Who the hell was she working with over there? Someone he knew? No, that wasn't the issue, not now. The silence stretched, but it wasn't uncomfortable despite their tension about the case. The only other person he'd routinely shared silence with was Heather, but she loved the quiet more than most; both their fathers appreciated children who were seen and not heard.

"So, the shelter…" he said.

"Seems one of their regular visitors—a model visitor by all accounts—relapsed a week after Heather's death. And nothing triggers relapse like stress…or guilt."

*That's it?* "A homeless addict relapsing?" he scoffed. "What are the odds?"

"I know, I know, but he'd cleaned up his act, found work —or so they assumed, because in the weeks before she died, he left the shelter every morning, well-dressed: khakis and button-downs and what they called 'clacky shoes' that woke the other residents when he got up early. Lots of folks wear uniforms like that, department stores, tech stores, even restaurants, but…"

The khakis. The wingtips. Could this man be the one Petrosky had seen on that snowy street, the man covered in Heather's blood? *The man who killed her.* If so, the money and the bank account might be unrelated; a homeless addict wouldn't be sleeping in a shelter if he had five years' worth of Heather's funds at his disposal. Maybe her death really had been about drugs, and Messinger had taken his funds back when he found out she was dead.

"Why didn't the detective on Heather's case know about some guy wearing clothes that matched Heather's killer? I know Mueller went to the shelter."

"The people at the shelter trust cops less than social workers—I'm there to offer services, not arrest them for loitering. And it's possible no one thought it was relevant unless the detective specifically asked about the outfit. This guy's only there a few days a week anyways—no one knows where he sleeps the rest of the time, or where he works. All I got was his name: Marius Brown."

"Marius Brown." Petrosky's own voice sounded spent,

hollow. He wanted to see the asshole in the flesh, but he couldn't just charge into the shelter and ambush him—there were procedures to follow, protocol.

Petrosky glanced at the time on the dash—it was after eight. Mueller wouldn't be at the precinct now. First thing in the morning, though, he'd tell Mueller about Marius Brown, and about Gene, Heather's friend from the shelter, the man Donald said had a thing for her. Gene had called with her schedules, but what was he really doing? Stalking her?

Maybe tomorrow he'd make progress. Maybe tomorrow he'd feel like he was doing something for Heather.

Maybe then he'd wake without Heather's blood on his hands.

**12**

———

THE SNOW TAPERED off as he drove home, but Petrosky's brain was stormy enough. Had Otis Messinger taken Heather's money now because he'd found out she was dead, or because he was one of the pair who'd killed her? Was Marius Brown the man with Heather's blood on his hands, her life soaking through his pants? Whether Messinger was the man in the truck or not, the man Petrosky had seen was the murderer—far too much blood on his clothes to have been overspray after someone else took a crowbar to Heather's skull.

The snow on the driveway was already devolving into a messy wet sludge. He parked but sat with his hand on the driver's door, the hairs on the back of his neck prickling. *Something's wrong.*

He scanned the icy road, looking for the glitter of eyes shining from the bushes, or a human form lurking behind a tree, but saw no one. No footprints on his lawn. The garage door was closed, the windows dark, the blinds drawn as he'd left them.

Petrosky squinted through the windshield, straining

against the glare off the ice on his porch. While the bushes nearest him were shrouded in white, the bushes on the far end of the property by the neighbor's drive were free of snow, as if they'd been brushed by someone climbing over them. And there *were* prints on the neighbor's drive. But neither of those things was what drew his attention now. A line of shadow darkened the base of his doorjamb—the door was cracked open.

Petrosky flew from the car, gun drawn, feet slipping on the icy top step, but he flung his hand out and righted himself on the railing. Breath panting around him, he froze on the porch, listening at the door, but heard only the steady *tick, tick* of the ice trickling off the roof, and his thundering heart. He nudged the door open.

The blazing headlights shone into the otherwise dark living room, making the green carpet all the more sickly where he could see it beneath the upended cushions and the papers that littered the floor. The vase his mother had given him—the only fancy thing he had in this place—was smashed, the shards of glass glittering like ice from the carpet.

Petrosky stilled, gun at the ready, then crept deeper into the gloom, past the kitchen, down the hall—shoving open the bathroom door as he passed it—then checked his bedroom, peered into the barren second bedroom. Empty. He lowered the gun. Whoever had been here was gone now.

He flicked on the lights, and blinked in the sudden harshness, so bright after the dim that it rang in his ears as if his retinas were screeching at him to turn off the lamps. But... no. There *was* a screeching sound—coming from outside. He ran back to the porch, glass crunching under his shoes, in time to see taillights disappear up the road. A truck. No...

*The* truck.

He ran from the house but slipped again on the icy top

step, and this time, he missed the railing, and then the world spiraled out of control until he landed, staring at the sky from a heap at the bottom of the stairs. Pain sang through his hip, his ankle, his elbow. Cursing, he scrambled to standing and hobbled to the car, leaping inside as the pickup swung around the far corner, out of his neighborhood. Headed for the freeway. He slammed the gearshift into reverse, and the car rolled backward to the street, but when he put it into drive again, a harsh grinding noise cut the air; the car felt lopsided, too, heavy and lower on his side. He stepped hard on the gas, jolting his neck as the car leapt forward, and the wheel caught the curb, the grinding louder now, far louder than the whining engine. *Fuck, no, no, no!*

The tires on his side were flat. Slashed.

He slammed his palms against the steering wheel and fumbled with the door handle—"Fuck!"—then flung the door wide and leapt from the car, the melting snow sliding under his feet, the front door clanging open—*I have to call Patrick!*—his shoes grinding broken glass into the living room carpet as he—*fuck.* The man, or men, who'd killed Heather had been *in his house.* Had they broken into Donald's place too? What were they looking for?

His shoes slipped on the kitchen linoleum, the surface slick with melted ice. He paused with his hand on the phone receiver.

You didn't kill a woman and then rob her place unless she had something you wanted—or something that could incriminate you. But why wait a month after her death? Unless the people who'd killed Heather found out about Linda's inquiries and thought Petrosky was onto them, and if that was the case...how would they know about the investigation?

Petrosky's brain felt fuzzy. His hands were numb. Nothing made sense. He let go of the phone and listened to the heavy *clunk* of the receiver falling into the cradle. If there was something here, he could find it himself. He sure didn't want Mueller digging through his shit…and hiding anything relevant.

Petrosky doubled back to close the front door and got a garbage bag from under the kitchen sink. For two hours, he scraped glass from the flattened green carpet, read then dumped torn papers into the garbage bag, righted upended side tables and dining chairs, dried melted snow from the tiles. When he got to the bedroom, he paused, staring at the rumpled sheets that he hadn't changed since Heather died. If she were still here, would they be arguing about what show to watch? Would she already be sick of his shit? She'd surely have made him wash the sheets.

He squared his shoulders, set the garbage bag on the floor, and knelt in the middle of the mess.

The bedroom only took half an hour, but the job drained the marrow from his bones. Every item he hadn't wanted to see—the fancy lotion he'd gotten for her just because, the jar smashed, the goo slippery and white on the floor, and her sweaters, every pair of her jeans—all of it on display to remind him of what had been. And what might have come next. Her notes for the wedding were still in their original position on the end table, though the plain lined notebook was now open to a page marked "Vows." Why had the intruder opened it? Whoever had done this hadn't cared about her dreams, about the goodness in her. They'd only wanted to destroy her.

The book trembled in his hands as though the pages were alive.

> *You've saved me in ways I never expected.*
> *I can't wait to spend a lifetime showing you how*
> *much I appreciate it.*

His heart was on fire. Tears stung his eyes. "What were you into, honey?" he asked the notebook. "What did they do to you?" The thing was hot in his hands. He tossed the book across the room, the pages rasping through the quiet. In the space behind the bed, he found the bottle—that was still there too. An hour later, with the Jack heavy in his blood and the bottle cold under his pillow, he slept.

## 13

"Ye can't just go in there and talk to Mueller," Patrick said, his muddy eyes flashing. "He's already been bitching that you're stepping on his toes, and the chief told ye to leave it be."

Petrosky stared through the windshield at the precinct. *I should have just walked in instead of stopping.* "All I did was ask him—"

"That's just it." Patrick tapped his fingers on the steering wheel. "Those fuckers don't like anyone second-guessing them, especially not some rookie."

"She was my fiancée."

"All the more reason for ye to stay the fuck away from it."

"Stay away? How can I just stay away? Could you stay away if it was your wife or your kid—"

"I get it, I do, but ye need to at least pretend to be lying low. So far, ye went and bitched at him without any new evidence, no proof, just guesses, and that sure as shite didn't help. Just made you look crazy."

*And reinforced their certainty that I don't belong on the case.* Patrick was right—he needed proof first. Petrosky wiped a hand down his face, the stubble on his cheeks catching his calloused fingers. He didn't need this shit, especially not after spending three hours this morning between waiting for the tow truck and watching the shop fix the filleted rubber that used to be his tires—if he'd had more than one spare, he could have done it faster his damn self. Petrosky's jaw clenched. He already regretted telling Patrick about Marius Brown, though he'd refused to name his source, and he still hadn't mentioned the break-in. Call it a gut thing or paranoia, but something was very wrong here, and he had no idea who to trust.

Patrick leveled a hard stare at him, one Petrosky had never seen before, dark and broody. Almost...cunning. "So what do we need to prove a link between this Marius Brown and the shooting? Right now, ye only have a hunch, but if ye were to see a picture of Brown..."

Petrosky frowned. They didn't have a picture, not yet, but they did have a composite of the man Petrosky had seen at Heather's crime scene. They could take that to the shelter; maybe someone could identify him. Yet, even if they confirmed *who* he was, the shelter workers had told Linda they didn't know *where* Marius Brown was. And if they went to the shelter with the composite sketch, they'd have to admit to Mueller and the chief that they'd interfered in the investigation. Again. Was there another way to ID him?

"You think Brown has a record?" Petrosky asked.

"Druggie, sleeping at the shelter, currently in the throes of relapse...probably. But narcotics isn't going to tell us anything—chief's orders. The chief already came to chat me up this morning, told me to keep yer ass away from the case. Bet he told the rumbly bloke in the file room too."

*Fuck the chief, fuck him in his stupid ear.* Petrosky sighed and drummed his fingers on the console. "So if we can't ask to see those cases, how are we going to make sure this Brown is our guy before we go talk to Mueller?"

"Who says we're going to ask, ye goat?"

"You keep your goat-fucking bullshit to yourself, Paddy."

Patrick grinned, Irish smug, but the humor in his irises had been sucked away. Irish *defiant*.

---

OFFICER JASON RHODES was on duty downstairs, sitting in a folding chair in front of a plywood desk, doing a crossword. Very constructive, not like there were bad guys to catch. Killers on the loose. Behind Rhodes, the hallway beckoned, a door on either side—one for evidence collection storage, the other leading to the file cabinets.

Petrosky's heart was in his throat. Rhodes raised his head and pushed a pair of little wire glasses up his beak nose. The twerp looked like a goddamn owl, but with a lazy eye that made him seem stupider than he probably was. Breaking in…that's what he and Patrick were doing, right? His chest heated. *Screw it*. So what if he lost this job? They'd been working him over from the moment he got here, and now they were letting Heather rot in a pile of file folders before shuffling her off to this dank hellhole for eternity. She deserved better. All families deserved better.

He'd never considered this part before, being on the receiving end of a cold case…the politics, the "give up and move on" mentality, the overworked detectives, the lack of funding to do more, to do better. The fact that doing better meant sneaking into this place instead of following orders… well, that was a bullshit side effect of bureaucracy. And he fucking hated bullshit.

Ol' Paddy was already leaning on the desk, his thick

fingers spread on the tabletop. Rhodes smiled—he did not look Petrosky's way.

"Patrick! You old sonofabitch, what've you been up to?"

Petrosky glanced at Patrick, but his partner remained planted in front of the desk. "Not too much—it's been too long, ye stook. Come get a coffee with me, and my partner can man the desk for ye."

*Is this how Patrick talks to the other cops?* It made him seem a little less "Irish defiant" and more like a wussy ass-kisser. There were likely worse ways to get ahead, but Petrosky couldn't think of any.

"Sorry, Pat, I can't leave my post. I have a million cases to finish putting away, and if I leave—"

"Yeah, I see how hard ye's working." Patrick gestured to the crossword, and Rhodes's cheeks went pink. "Don't be a knob. Not like the files're going to run away—they'll be safe with Ed, here." He smiled, but gooseflesh prickled on Petrosky's arms. Man was a damn fine liar. Just like Heather had been.

But if Petrosky thought she was just a liar, why was he risking his job for her?

*Because someone turned her into whatever she became. And because I love her.*

Rhodes cast Petrosky a sidelong glance. "It's... I can't let him in."

"Jesus, Mary, and Joseph, he can figure out how to get people to sign the paper."

"No, it's not that, the chief said—"

"The chief has to say that, does it every time someone loses a family member, right? Just a precaution."

The man's face softened as he looked back at Petrosky—pity. Petrosky bristled. *We should have come in through a fucking window.*

"He's okay, Rhodes. Ye have my word on it, and ain't

nothing more pure than the word of an Irishman," Patrick said, and it came out "Oye-rishman."

Rhodes sighed. "All right. One cup of coffee." He glanced once at the file room and back at Patrick. "I never really liked the chief anyway."

Ass kisser or not, Ol' Paddy's tactics were effective.

Rhodes stood, and Petrosky took his spot. He had twenty minutes, probably less. But Rhodes stood there a moment, eyeing the table, then the file room door again.

*Twenty minutes from when he* leaves. *Get it together, Petrosky don't be a fucking dumbass goat.* Or whatever Patrick would say.

His partner cast him one last look as he headed up the stairs with Rhodes. Petrosky listened for the *thunk* of the door closing, the *clack* of the latch, and ran for the file room.

---

THE ROOM SMELLED like stale cigarette smoke—menthol, horrible shit, but his mouth watered. On the back wall, a cheap plastic clock *tick-tick*ed away the minutes above the center row of chest-high file cabinets. The side walls were also lined with metal drawers.

Marius Brown. Who might be the man he'd seen in the street. The man covered in Heather's blood.

The man who'd killed her—and had gotten away.

But why had he killed her? The drug thing made the most sense, just like it made sense for Messinger to have taken his money back once she was dead. But it didn't *feel* right. There had been two people in that truck. Two. Brown might have killed her, but he'd had a partner. And they'd paged Heather that day, called her into the darkness behind the school. That didn't feel like just drugs. Her murder felt planned, premeditated, which meant there was a motive. A reason.

Petrosky headed for the side wall, where the filing cabinets were lined up in alphabetical order. Dust mites irritated his nose, and he stifled a sneeze. Marius Brown...Brown... The first cabinet had "Aa-Ak" Sharpied on a thin strip of masking tape. He walked down the row until he found "Bo-Bz." He grabbed the drawer and yanked. It stuck fast. The filing cabinet was locked.

*Fuck.*

He ran back to the front desk...empty. *That ass didn't leave the keys?* But of course he hadn't—Rhodes wasn't willing to risk his job by leaving a way for Petrosky to sneak in.

Petrosky jerked open the desk drawers—pens, paper, another book of crosswords. In the right drawer beneath a package of Scotch tape lay a Swiss Army knife, the metal cool against his palm. The clock on the wall read 9:22: he'd already wasted three minutes.

Knife in hand, he returned to the file room and slipped the blade into the top of the drawer, just behind the locking mechanism. The lock did not budge. He eased it left, then right, wriggling the blade against the metal, recalling the old Buick his father used to have, the one that had never had a working lock; his father had to pick it every time he parked somewhere unsavory.

Eight minutes left. *Fuck.*

His father would never have taken so long. Petrosky should have spent more time practicing. *Yeah, right, because I'll definitely use a Swiss Army knife to break into police files in the future.*

Then: *snap.* The lock clicked open, and he slid the drawer out, closed the blade, and slipped the knife into his pocket. He flipped through the files, three, six, nine, twenty, twenty-five, Boole, Boscowitz, Briar...

Five minutes left.

He flipped another file. *There.* Marius Brown. Patrick had

been right about him having a record unless it was another Marius Brown. He ripped out the folder, accidentally pulling the one in front of it, too, those pages flapping as they fell like a million angry moths had invaded the file room.

From the hall, something squawked, and he froze—the door to the basement. They were back. He grabbed the file he'd dropped, trying to right it, then settled for shoving sheet after sheet into the manila folder, crumpling the pages as he wrestled them into the back of the cabinet.

He straightened and tore open Brown's folder. No murder raps yet, just charges for possession—opioids and OxyContin. The mug shot showed the man, gaze dull and dead and... *It's him.* Petrosky would have recognized Heather's killer anywhere, even without the truck sitting behind him, without the khakis, without Heather's blood covering his arms. Her dead face bubbled to the surface of his brain, and despair rose in his chest; he stamped it back down. Footsteps sounded on the stairs, closer now. He glanced once more at the case in his hand before stuffing it beneath his jacket. Last known address, a place where Heather had spent a few days every week delivering clothes and making meals. The homeless shelter. Full of people just trying to survive.

## 14

"AND you just happened to see a picture of this guy?" Mueller's elbows were planted on the desk, one hand still clutching his morning cup of coffee.

"Yes. I saw a photo at the shelter when I went to drop off some of Heather's clothes," Petrosky said. "One of those walls full of smiling folks, trying to sell the place—like anyone there needs a reason besides the beds."

Mueller's eyes narrowed; he knew Petrosky was lying. But to his credit, he merely nodded. "I thought you were full of shit when you walked in here this morning, but…"

Petrosky waited for him to say more, but Mueller sat back and sipped at his coffee. Returned the mug to the desktop.

*Come on, you bastard, I just waited for an hour while you dicked around on the phone.* "But what?"

"Bank says that Marius Brown came into some money the day after Heather Ainsley died—a ton of money. Nearly fifty grand."

Fifty grand—five years' worth of mortgage and home health aide payments? Not only had Marius Brown killed

Heather, someone had paid him to do it…with Heather's money. Petrosky swallowed back bile along with the unrelenting rage bubbling in his gut. Maybe he should tell Mueller about the money withdrawn from Heather's account, about Messinger—but no. The man had enough to start investigating. Petrosky would hold that tidbit back for the moment Mueller wanted to let the case go cold again.

Mueller gestured to the stairs. "Why don't you go out on the roads with your partner there?"

*If he thinks I'm going to just let him handle it—*

"That's your beat, right? The streets around the shelter? I'll need backup if things go wrong, and if you happen to be around, there isn't much the chief can say, conflict of interest or no."

Wait, Mueller was…giving him an in on the case? "I can do that," Petrosky said quickly. Maybe Mueller wasn't as much of a pig-fucker as he'd thought.

---

THE DAY WAS frigid but sunny, the brittle wind in the parking lot burning his cheeks like gusts of flame. Petrosky put the car into drive and eased onto the road behind Mueller's car. Sweat stuck his uniform collar to the back of his neck despite the frosty breeze.

"You're sure he said to follow him?" Patrick squinted at the road.

*Nope.* The slush on the streets made a wet slapping sound against the sides of his car—*flup, flup, flup*—yesterday's ice on the curbs glistening in the brilliant sunlight. Petrosky glanced over; Patrick was frowning at the windshield. Petrosky turned away. He still hadn't said a word about the robbery to Patrick. Twice he'd opened his mouth to tell him, but each time a tightness in his chest had held him back.

Instead of considering what that meant, he kept his eyes on Mueller's ten-year-old Dodge as the detective pulled into the shelter.

Petrosky switched on the walkie, hoping it would stay silent. Mueller had said to drive their beat, and he'd call for backup if Marius Brown was there, but any call that came into this area might be their responsibility too. A car door slammed. Petrosky's heart rate increased as Mueller's gaze flicked over to Petrosky's car and away again, and then Mueller was walking briskly over the salted lot toward the ice-crusted shelter. The place wasn't huge: maybe two thousand square feet of open space, bunk beds stacked wall-to-wall, volunteers changing sheets or making food. It'd be hard to hide in there. The shelter was locked up like a vault at night—most places down here were—but this time of morning, people would be eating or getting ready to clear out. Hopefully they hadn't missed Marius.

Moments later, Mueller reemerged, frowning, and slid behind his wheel once more. "Where to now?" Patrick muttered.

Petrosky put the car in gear and followed the detective through the thawing city. He didn't remember pulling out his cigarettes, but suddenly there was one in his mouth, the hard, grating cold of the lighter against his thumb, the smoke in his nostrils. The slushy street crawled past on either side, the sun so blinding against the icy mounds of snow topping the curbs that Petrosky almost missed Mueller making a hard right into a lot. A blast of cold air chilled his cheek, the side facing Patrick, but though the window stayed down, Pat had the decency to keep his mouth shut.

The sign above the neon green building screamed: *BIG BOX APPLIANCE*. The red brick building beside it had boards covering most of the front windows, and the windows without boards were gaping holes. No glass.

*The fuck you doing, Mueller?* Petrosky stopped beside Mueller's unmarked car and stared at the front of the building, his lips tight around the cig, inhaling like a vacuum.

Mueller wasn't inside long—he came stomping back out to the lot less than five minutes later, but instead of heading for his own ride, he stalked over to theirs. "Marius Brown works here, according to Jerry, the shelter janitor."

Petrosky frowned. All this time and no one had a clue where Brown worked, but suddenly this Jerry knew exactly where to find him?

"He got in to work at eight," Mueller said, "but got a page about thirty minutes later and said he had to run a 'quick errand.' Sounds like it's a usual thing for him—he's probably dealing."

Petrosky glanced at the dashboard clock: nine fifteen. Only forty-five minutes since Brown left. "I'm shocked he came in at all with that cash in his account. Must have taken a detour on his way back to work." Unless Brown knew they were coming to get him. If the guy was running, they'd put out an APB, find him before he got too far. Petrosky shoved his door open.

"I'll call it in, get units on the lookout," Mueller said as if reading his mind. "But if someone else paged him, they might have picked him up—sounded like he went out the front and not the back where the employee lot is."

"Does he even have a vehicle?" Unlikely, or he'd be sleeping in it. Petrosky squinted at the building, then at the alley that ran between the appliance store and the red brick monstrosity beside it. "Might be worth checking the employee lot anyway." They should at least look around before calling it in; they could wait in the lot in case Brown showed. Petrosky was in his uniform, but neither of them had driven a marked police car, so Brown wouldn't know they were here until he went inside—and then it'd be too late to dodge them.

Mueller eyed the building again, then nodded.

The melting snow squelched beneath Petrosky's rubber soles, the wind crisp and cool against his face as they stepped into the shade of the buildings. The narrow alley was just wide enough for a car. The appliance store's lime paint was peeling here and there, revealing scars of gray cinderblock on their left, and the abandoned three-story red-brick building hulked on their right; no windows on either side, no hint from here as to what the buildings contained. From three stories up, the pale sun beamed through the rectangle that marked the rooflines.

At the end of the alley was a cracked square concrete pad with room for no more than four cars. A Pontiac Firebird with rust around the rear well sat parked to their left, at the mouth of the alley. In the farthest spot, beside the rear entrance to the shop, was an orange Pinto, beetle-like, the back end peeking from behind a wood-paneled station wagon. Petrosky stepped toward the back of the lot, where a low brick wall separated them from a similar parking lot beyond. "If he doubled back and hopped this wall instead of heading up the street, we might have witnesses to tell us which way…"

Petrosky stopped walking.

Behind him, Mueller whispered, "Shit."

A pair of wingtips, the same as those the killer had worn the night he murdered Heather, poked around the Pinto's back tires, toes pointed up. Petrosky stepped past the car.

Marius Brown lay on the pavement, a hole in the center of his chest, his shirt soaked in blood. His eyes stared blankly at the sky.

Had no one heard the gunshot? Then again, the walls were made of brick, and only half these buildings were occupied. Anyone who did hear would have thought it was a car backfiring. People preferred the sunnier explanation.

"Is this the man who killed Heather Ainsley?" Mueller said from behind him, and his voice sounded awfully far away, as if he were speaking through a tunnel.

"That's him," Petrosky said, and his voice, too, seemed to be coming to his ears from a distance.

They were all quiet for a moment, then Mueller spoke: "This ain't right."

*About goddamn time.*

---

PATRICK DROVE them back to the station, Petrosky's thoughts so loud he could barely hear the whine of the engine, let alone focus on the road.

Petrosky was glad Brown was dead—served him right. His only reservation was that they couldn't question the man, find out why he'd killed Heather and who his ski-masked partner in the truck was—the man who'd shot Patrick. Petrosky closed his eyes against the blinding sun that streamed through the windshield.

So what now? Heather's death had to be more than a drug deal gone bad, or Marius Brown would still be alive. Maybe Brown was murdered by his partner in the car; maybe that cop-shooting mystery man had thought Brown was going to expose their crime or sell him out in exchange for a lighter sentence. Maybe that same person had broken into Petrosky's house, too, searching for anything that would implicate him in Heather's death. Had to be this Otis Messinger, right? Messinger was the only other person who had access to Heather's funds, and he'd put her cash into Brown's account the day after she died. If they looked at

Marius Brown's statements now, would they find his sudden influx of cash had been wiped out as well?

Petrosky's blood boiled, rage forcing away that painful, lonely ache. Vengeance was a bad thing; he'd learned this early in his military career. It made you reckless. But justice…that was worth fighting for, even if the two were flip sides of the same coin. Petrosky had to figure out exactly what he was dealing with—and who. He opened his eyes.

The shelter. He had to go back. Maybe he'd bring Linda. She seemed to have a better grasp on this case than any of them: connections at the shelter, connections to the people involved, and he knew she wasn't complicit in the killings; she wouldn't have reopened the case for them if she'd had something to do with it.

"You want to get a bite?"

Patrick's voice pulled Petrosky from his head back to the car, the *slishhhh* of the tires over the road halting as the car stopped in front of the precinct. "Not now. Have a few errands to run."

"Ye sure? Sounds like Mueller is going to snag Heather's friend from the shelter, Gene Carr, for questioning—he knew Marius Brown too. We can get takeout and watch."

Petrosky cocked his head. "How do you even know that?"

"I pulled a few strings." Patrick nodded, but his lips were turned down at the corners, eyes tight.

Patrick could pull strings to watch questioning, but they had to break in to get files? Whose ass did ol' Paddy kiss with those big Irish lips of his? *Maybe he just played nice instead of telling the chief to fuck off.* Politics.

"I'll be back in forty-five minutes," Petrosky said. "Mueller didn't look like he was in a hurry to leave the scene, and the shelter employees move between buildings before lunch—Heather'd use my car to pick up donations from nearby churches. Gene Carr might be harder to track down than Mueller realizes."

But that wasn't the reason he was leaving. Messinger was their best lead, and Petrosky didn't want to sit around until Mueller got back from the crime scene.

He was done waiting.

## 15

———

THE RECEPTIONIST at the social work office eyed him with the exhausted-bored expression of a tollbooth operator on a double shift.

"Is Linda Davies available?" Petrosky raised a plastic bag of takeout.

She furrowed her brows, then picked up the receiver from the desk. "Linda? Someone to see you."

Why was he here again? He didn't have a specific reason to think that Linda knew more than she'd already told him, but somehow coming here had *felt* like the most reasonable option. She'd take a look at the case with him, help him figure it out. Plus, she understood this pain. And she'd learned to push past it.

Linda emerged from the back hallway. Her jaw dropped when she saw Petrosky.

"I hope you like Chinese—chicken or shrimp, your choice."

Linda glanced at the receptionist who was now staring with unmasked interest, then motioned for him to follow.

"I hope it's okay that I stopped by unannounced. I figured lunch was the best time to catch you without a client."

She nodded. "You got lucky. Most days I eat in my car between home visits."

"But not today?" *Why not today?* She shrugged. Seemed this Tuesday consisted of many strange events—like discovering your fiancée's murderer with a fresh hole in his chest.

He followed Linda down a short beige hallway and into a tiny office of the same color, the blandness of the walls broken by framed college degrees to the left of her desk and a large painting of sunflowers on the back wall beside the window. The blinding sun had vanished while he was in the Chinese restaurant; it was snowing again.

Linda grabbed a stack of files to make room for the containers on her scarred pine desk. She set a squat vase of fake pink roses on the floor by her feet. "Did you talk to Brown?"

"He's dead." Petrosky set the last wax container on the desktop and looked up in time to see Linda's eyes widen.

"What? How can that…oh my god."

"Who was your contact at the shelter? Today everyone seemed to know an awful lot about where Brown worked." He pushed plastic utensils in her direction, a peace offering— his words had come out harsher than he'd intended.

She unwrapped a fork, then grabbed the takeout container closest to her. "That's weird. Did you talk to Sheila?"

He dropped his gaze and opened the other box. Steam laced with salt and MSG slapped him in the face. "The detective talked to someone named Jerry, not Sheila."

"Ah, that guy usually works the night shift." She stabbed a piece of orange chicken.

But Jerry and Sheila weren't the reasons he'd come. He

pulled the Szechwan shrimp toward him, the spicy air stinging his nostrils. "Listen, Linda, maybe we're going about this all wrong. We're looking for clues in the crime scene, in Heather's murder, but...what about this man who spent a decade giving her money? He's the key here—even broke into my house to make sure she hadn't left evidence there... or...well, fuck I dunno."

Linda froze with her fork poised above the rice. "Someone broke into your—"

"Just hear me out. Marius Brown kills Heather with another man in the truck. Heather's account gets cleaned out the day after she dies...and that money immediately goes into Brown's account."

She dropped her fork and snatched it back up. "Marius... they paid him to...wow."

"Then today, someone kills Marius."

"I—"

"Messinger is the key to this, Linda, the one we have to find."

She exhaled, hard—frustrated. "I tried. I asked around at the bank, looked for Messinger. The cops might do better, but I asked the same questions they would have."

He scooped a forkful of shrimp and rice into his maw and chewed, then swallowed. "I need to know what type of man pays teenagers to, you know...abuse them. Or maybe she ran drugs? I don't know what she was doing, just that it had to be illegal for the kind of cash she was pulling in." *Maybe she was a hitman like Brown.* He almost laughed.

"Well, paying kids to run drugs is hardly new—you see it a lot in the inner cities, gangs. As for the type of man who might pay teenage girls for sex, the whole fashion industry is built around youth. Shave your pubic hair, look like a twelve-year-old, be sexy; that's mainstream." She forked another bite of chicken but frowned at it instead of putting it in her mouth.

He leaned back from the desk and rested his fork hand on his knee. "This guy is different—more than just a pervy middle-aged jackass." And Messinger had to be older if he'd had money ten years ago when Heather first started paying for her father's house.

Linda set the fork down. "You're looking for a profile."

"I guess I am."

"You have department shrinks for that."

"I'd like to hear it from you." Because…he trusted her—she had *wanted* to help.

She sat back in her chair, and the wooden legs squeaked. Linda frowned. "We just don't have a lot to go on. Whether he was using her for sex, or paying her to sell drugs, or even hiring her out…there's a huge difference in profiles." *Hiring her out.* Petrosky swallowed hard to avoid gagging.

Linda was still talking. "What we do know is that he's careful—he took his time. He might have paid into her account for months before he asked her to do anything questionable, conditioning her, brainwashing her…getting her to trust him. Which she did. She never told a soul that he even existed."

The words lodged in his ribs. "But killing her…why now, if they've been connected for a decade? And why murder her out in the open?" But Heather wasn't an idiot; if she'd suspected she was in danger, as Linda seemed to think, she wouldn't have met this guy somewhere private. Though if she'd met him on that street…he could have carried her farther behind the school.

"That's just it—we have no way of knowing why she died, Ed, not for sure. Marius Brown might have been paid to do it, but—"

"Brown was a hitman. A *hitman*. Messinger lured her out

there and let Brown kill her—he didn't just give Brown that money the following day for no reason. What did she do to deserve that?" His voice was rising, and he clutched the fork in his hand so tightly the plastic bit into the meat of his palm.

Linda leaned forward again. "We just don't know." Her voice was almost a whisper. But there was a nervous glitter in her eyes, and when she looked down, he was certain she was holding back.

"We might not know for sure," he said. "But guess. Please."

She took a deep breath and let it out slowly, keeping her gaze on the desk. "If I'd spent a decade giving a woman money for something illegal, I'd worry she'd tell her new cop husband about me."

Needles bored into the back of his skull. Linda was right —nothing had changed for Heather in the decade before her death, nothing to make her "employer" uneasy. Nothing except Petrosky. Maybe this Messinger had found out she was marrying him and thought she might spill her secrets. Maybe she'd even tried to get out herself.

But breaking up is hard to do.

"Might even be old fashioned jealousy," Linda continued, facing him once more. "If Messinger kept her to himself all those years, spent all that time conditioning her, paying her...I don't think he'd want to share her with a husband." She speared a broccoli stalk like she wished it was their suspect's balls.

"Okay, so maybe he's jealous, got worried she'd run her mouth. Either way...how do I catch him now? What would make him come out of hiding?" But the guy wasn't hiding— they just didn't know who they were looking for.

She shoved a bite into her mouth, then tapped her plastic fork against the desktop for a few moments. "If you had a suspect, you could push him, aggravate him, see if he slipped up. It wouldn't take much—he's already freaked enough to break into your house."

*If you had a suspect.* The wall clock *tick, tick, ticked* like the ice on the parking lot the night he'd ambushed Linda outside her office. Thirty seconds passed. Forty. He cleared his throat to break the silence. "So, my only option is to stress him out once I figure out who he is?" Super useful. Last time he tried this psychology shit.

"I wouldn't advocate antagonizing murder suspects, but if he wanted you dead, he'd have tried to kill you already."

"I think he did try to kill me." Petrosky set his fork in the rice container and stared past Linda out the snow-covered window, then at the adjacent painting of orange and gold sunflowers, so fucking happy like they knew the snow wouldn't last. But it might. "My partner was shot the night Heather died—the truck was just idling in the road like it was waiting for us, Marius Brown standing there covered in Heather's blood, and the guy in the passenger seat, aiming a gun out the back window..."

"Marius just stood there?" She frowned.

"Looked high as shit, yeah, but he sure started moving once his partner shot Patrick. He could have been faking, trying to distract us." And it had worked.

"What if he wasn't?"

"Wasn't what?"

"High. Or faking. Take your pick."

"He was covered in her blood. Covered. Far too much for it to have splattered from someone else hitting her, no matter how close he was standing. He had to have been down on the ground, working her over himself. And they *paid* him, Linda. Why would they do that if he hadn't killed her?" An image of Brown flashed behind Petrosky's eyelids, Heather's brain matter on Brown's hands, her blood on his khakis, almost black in the moonlight, the gelatinous mess sliding from Brown's fingers, the wet *plip* of gore hitting the street.

Linda shook her head. "It *is* weird that they were still there when you arrived. And with the break-in…" She leaned toward him, her gaze hard. "Maybe someone wanted you dead that night, but now he just wants to make sure there's no one left to tell you anything. If you knew who he was, he'd be in cuffs already. And it's riskier to kill a cop than murder someone no one cares about."

The heaviness in his gut moved into his chest, crushing his breastbone, the few bites of Chinese souring in his belly. "I care. I cared about her."

Linda dropped her fork in the orange chicken and walked around the desk to sit beside him. She laid a hand on his arm. "I didn't mean—"

"No…you're right." His voice cracked, just the tiniest bit, but enough for him to want to punch himself in the throat. "It's bullshit, the way it works, the way no one cares unless you have…unless you're worth more."

"I know, and people like us are stuck in the trenches—seeing the folks the rest of the world forgets. But it's okay, Ed." His name didn't sound so bad on her tongue, and suddenly his ache for Heather seemed to multiply inside him; he could feel her in that room with them, and his hands tensed with the desire to hold her, to listen to her soft breath, to brush her curls from her face one more time. Tears smarted behind his eyes, and he swiped at his cheeks, turning his face away. Linda squeezed his arm, a soft, gentle pressure near the back of his wrist.

"I understand, Ed. I lost someone too. It never goes away, but it does get easier, I promise."

For a moment, he could smell Heather's flowery perfume, the gardenia she used in her hair, feel the warmth of her, too, but it passed as Linda released him. "It's hard down here in the trenches," she muttered.

He'd been face down in the dirt, literally or figuratively, his whole life. And he was tired of it. He needed to do something...good. There had to be something better.

## 16

GENE CARR WAS A SNIVELING little twit with a face like a gnome and brown eyes that matched the hair at his temples—an older fellow, fifty at least. Vaguely familiar, too, though Petrosky couldn't place him. Probably from the shelter.

Mueller stood on his side of the metal table, fingers spread on the surface like they were waiting for Gene Carr to do something stupid so Mueller could wrap those beefy digits around his suspect's throat.

"How well did you know Heather Ainsley?" Mueller barked.

Gene's lip trembled, and he shook his head. "Just from work, sir."

"Sounds like you wanted to know her a little better than she'd let you, is that right?"

"I...I..." Carr shook his head again. "No."

"Really? Because I have a statement from her father that says otherwise."

"From Donald?" His eyes widened, and his knuckles went white on the tabletop. "Donald said that? Please, I just...I only called to make sure she was coming to work, and then one night, we were just going to go dancing, I swear!"

Petrosky almost smiled, remembering the first time he visited Heather at Donald's house. The old guy had been sitting in his wheelchair by the front door polishing his old army rifle, telling a heartwarming story about the good ol' days when he'd singlehandedly sniped three dozen men in an hour. But his hands had been shaking too much for Petrosky to take him seriously. It seemed Gene had met Donald before disease had robbed the old man of his coordination.

"You and Heather went dancing?"

"We were supposed to. It was like…eight, nine months ago. April maybe? But she never showed. I asked her out a few times after that, but she always said she was busy."

April. That was when Petrosky had picked her up on the street. Had she been on her way to meet this tool? But if that were the case, why wouldn't she tell him she was going dancing instead of letting him pick her up on suspicion of prostitution? He'd even asked if she worked at the massage parlor up the block, and she'd just stared. *She must have been meeting Gene a different night.*

"Sounds like you were pretty interested in her schedule," Mueller continued. "To keep calling a girl who wasn't inter-ested…that seem like a normal thing to do?"

"I haven't done it in months!" he said, and when Mueller cocked his head: "The calling her, I mean. She kept turning me down, so I stopped."

"Because it made you angry, Gene?"

He shook his head. "I wasn't angry. Look at me." He gestured to his paunchy middle. "What would a beautiful girl like her want with a guy like me?" He shrugged, but his face was pained, eyes so sincere that Petrosky…almost believed him.

"You know a guy named Otis Messinger?" Mueller said.

The name on Heather's bank account, the person who'd drained off her funds after her death. Petrosky had been uneasy after lunch when he'd filled Mueller in on Messinger—he didn't want to show his whole hand too soon—but the thought that her murder might be partially his fault... He needed to do anything he could to help close the case.

"No." Gene relaxed his hands, and the color flooded back into his knuckles.

"Marius Brown, a guy I hear you know pretty well from the shelter, came into a pile of money after Heather died. It almost looks like someone paid him to kill her." Mueller bent until he was practically nose to nose with the other man, and Gene's face went ashen. "What will I find if I check your accounts?" Though they already knew the answer to that: Gene's financial records were abysmal. The man had filed for bankruptcy two years ago after his divorce, and his bank accounts showed a constant battle to pay his bills. And working at the shelter didn't pay shit. Gene had to be doing something on the side to make ends meet, but it probably had nothing to do with Heather.

"Where were you on Thursday the week before Thanksgiving?"

The day Heather was killed.

"I...I have no idea. Home?"

"Alone?"

Gene nodded. "I usually am. Since the divorce, well..."

Mueller snorted. "Not much of an alibi."

"I didn't know I needed one, sir." Now Gene shifted, and something stole over his face, tightening his lips. He lowered his hands beneath the table. "Am I under arrest?"

"No, you're not." Mueller leaned closer. "Not yet, anyway."

Gene stood. "Then, I'm going home." His eyes glittered defiantly like a cornered raccoon who had lost the desire to take anyone's shit. He headed around the table, staying as close to the wall—and as far from Mueller—as he could.

Petrosky left the observation area and strode toward the lobby. Gene knew his rights better than most innocent people. Maybe he'd known he might be called in for questioning. Maybe he knew he should be under arrest. But without any evidence to link Gene to Heather's death, or to Heather's money, or to suggest a relationship with Marius Brown, they couldn't keep him there. All they knew was that he was a friend of Heather's, a friend who used to call her incessantly, but that wasn't illegal. They couldn't even connect him to the call made to Brown this morning; according to the shelter staff, Gene hadn't made any calls or left work either. But still...something wasn't right about this guy.

The door to the interrogation room squealed open, and Gene exited, running a hand over his hair. He saw Petrosky and froze.

Petrosky smiled, hoping it looked predatory.

The man stayed put, hands clenching and unclenching at his hips, then took off for the exit, practically running.

Petrosky fought the urge to race after the man and kick the shit out of him until he spilled whatever the fuck he knew. *No, not now. Get control of yourself.* But shit, he could almost taste it, could almost smell the iron of the man's blood, could almost feel Gene's jaw breaking beneath his knuckles, hear the impact like crackling tinder. Except Gene wasn't the one he needed to hurt. If Petrosky found the man responsible for Heather's death...god help them both.

# 17



*WHAT ARE YOU DOING, Petrosky?*

He shifted in the seat of his Grand Am and stared at the homeless shelter, the concrete building dark beneath the charcoal sky, the light from the streetlamp glossy against the skin of dirty gray snow on the roof. He should have gone home to get some rest after Gene Carr left the station, but adrenaline sang through his blood, so electric that the thought of sleeping made him want to crawl out of his skin. He might have gone to the bank to look for new leads on Messinger, but then he'd have to explain it once Mueller found out. Like it or not, as far as the brass was concerned, this wasn't his case—he had to play it cool or at least quiet.

So instead, he'd clocked out and driven to Gene's home, circled the man's block, looking for anything out of the ordinary—*a pickup truck, perhaps?*—making up excuses in his head in case anyone caught him. Stealing Gene's address from Mueller's file would surely be frowned upon. Petrosky didn't believe Gene had anything to do with Heather's death, but the man had been far too nervous to be completely in the dark—did he know something? Someone at the shelter had to. That was why Petrosky had followed Gene back to the shelter for his night shift, and that was why he was still sitting here three hours later.

Mueller should fucking be here himself, watching this place. Marius Brown had stayed here. Heather had volunteered here. And someone had paged Heather from the pay phone in front of this building the day she died. Clearly, the shelter was a common link, and Petrosky was going to find out precisely what that connection meant. Did Otis Messinger have a relationship to the shelter? Messinger didn't own it—the shelter was a government-funded non-profit operated by a local mental health agency—but there were lots of patrons, lots of volunteers…and lots of ways for a man to sneak about unnoticed. The gray facade of the shelter shone like a beacon.

*Don't be a dodgy bastard, ye'll lose yer badge.* Patrick's words echoed in his head. For a guy who'd been so gung-ho about breaking into the file room, he'd sure changed his tune once they actually had Mueller's attention. But Petrosky wasn't in Mueller's crosshairs now, not here cloaked in the pitch dark in the back of this parking lot, well beyond the reach of the lone streetlamp.

He squinted in his rearview mirror at the pay phone across the street and took a bite of his cheeseburger—soggy now. He'd never been a fan of fast food, but damn if it didn't come in handy for sitting in a parking lot all night.

After the food was gone, the ashtray filled slowly. His stomach soured with grease and sugar. Three o'clock came and went. Four. He leaned back against the headrest, sipping cold coffee from a thermos he'd bought from home.

At four thirty, another car appeared on the road—no, not a car. Bigger. He hunched down in his seat when the passing headlights lit up the interior of his car…no, not passing. Turning into the lot.

He slid lower, peering through the side-view mirror as the vehicle passed his car—a van, white, no windows. A bumper sticker reading "FOOD GIFTS" was affixed to the side.

FOOD GIFTS. Was that one of the organizations providing food to the shelters? The van parked in front of the building. The driver climbed out.

FOOD GIFTS. Something tingled between his shoulder blades, and he jerked forward, nearly hitting his head on the steering wheel. The bumper sticker, half torn off the side of the pickup truck—*OD...FTS...*

His heartbeat throbbed in his temples. Petrosky had played with the letters from that bumper sticker for days after Heather died, desperate to know what it meant. And while he'd run through the names of nearby businesses, he hadn't considered do-gooder operations, hadn't considered charities. He should have. He should have done a lot of things.

But he could do some of those things now.

He checked the time—Gene wasn't due to get off for two more hours. Petrosky watched, sipping his cold coffee, heart racing, as the van driver unloaded crates. When the man got back behind the wheel, Petrosky smashed the last of his cigarette into the ashtray. The van turned onto the main road. Petrosky started his car.

# 18

Food Gifts headquarters was located ten miles outside Ash Park, on a street with potholes so deep you could crack your axles. Petrosky followed cautiously, giving the van a wide berth, and passed the driveway when the van turned into a warehouse parking lot.

He hooked a U-turn a few hundred feet past the building, then doubled back into the parking lot and rolled to a stop beside a cherry-red Mustang. Pretty. Maybe too pretty for employees of a food bank, but what did he know? He was just a flatfoot, but he'd be damned if he was calling Mueller. Who knew what he'd miss while Mueller was fucking around trying to get here? And Petrosky didn't need the chief on his ass either.

The wind bit close as he got out, grating against his unshaven face—with his uncombed hair and the sweatpants he'd worn to sit in the car all night, he probably looked like someone in search of food himself. All the better. He paused on the walk in front of the building as a man in blue jean overalls and a windbreaker far too light for the icy wind entered through the side door. Petrosky followed, head low.

The inside of Food Gifts was one enormous room, like the shelter, but here they housed provisions instead of people. Floor-to-ceiling shelving lined each of the four walls, and a pallet jack sat near the center. There was a table along the back, too, and four employees that he could see, all in sweatshirts and jeans and knit caps.

"Can I help you?"

Petrosky turned to see a short, slim woman walking toward him—eighteen, tops, with a ring in her eyebrow and a thick yellow scrunchie on her wrist. She had dark hair and light eyes like Heather. "I'm with the Ash Park Police Department. Just had a few questions about your organization. What's your name?"

She stopped a few feet away. "Shandi Lombardi."

"Lombardi? Italian?" He tried to smile—if he put her at ease, she'd be more likely to talk to him.

"Something like that." She tapped her foot, sheathed in a tiny green sneaker that looked like it belonged to a doll.

*Enough bullshit, Jesus Christ.* Mueller sure hadn't been polite during his interrogation of Gene Carr, and the detective was trained for this. Petrosky cleared his throat. "Did you know Marius Brown?"

The girl's eyes widened, then narrowed, and her cheek twitched. His hackles rose.

"Should I know who that is?"

*She's lying.* He wasn't sure how he knew that, but he was positive—felt it deep in his gut like shards of shrapnel. "Marius Brown was a frequent visitor to the shelter on Breveport, so some of the workers thought your organization might have had contact with him. We also have reason to believe that a truck driven by Marius was affiliated with Food Gifts."

"You mean a van?"

"Nope. A blue pickup. With one of your bumper stickers on the side."

She squinted. "We don't have trucks here, just the vans. But anyone who makes a donation over twenty-five dollars gets a bumper sticker." She cocked her head. "Why are you looking for this guy anyway?"

"He's dead."

Her foot tapped overtime on the concrete floor, but her face didn't change. Nervous maybe, though not upset about Brown. She reminded Petrosky of a soldier in his platoon— they'd woken up to find him torturing a camel, rubbing salt into its eyes, the poor animal's legs severed at the knee joint. Oh, how it had screamed. Petrosky had shot it in the head. It was one kill that hadn't kept him awake at night.

"You can ask around, but I'm not sure anyone else can tell you more, Officer Petrosky."

He froze. "I don't remember telling you my name."

"I must have guessed." But she looked down at the floor as if she were ashamed, and now he could see the tremble in her hands, the vein throbbing at her throat. She was lying, but she was terrified. And her knowing his name told him more than anything else she'd said—she knew who he was...who Heather was. Did she know Heather's killer, or Otis Messinger, or the person who'd broken into his house? Did she need his help too? *What do you know?*

"Listen, you seem like a sweet kid."

She raised her chin, and one corner of her mouth twitched up—*like Heather, like Heather*—but her defiant eyes stayed the same: blue pools, deep enough to drown him.

"If someone is hurting you, making you uncomfortable...I can help."

"I'm fine." But the dark determination in her gaze was gone, replaced by thinly veiled panic.

"I'm sure you are fine. But see, I was talking to Gene this morning, and—"

"What's he have to do with anything?" she snapped.

*I was right.* "I'm not sure yet, but Gene seemed pretty nervous, just like you are, and I'd like to know why that is."

The muscles in her jaw went rigid. "I have no idea what you're talking about." Her gaze had softened, anxiety and confusion, not like the camel killer—that guy's eyes had been as dead as stone.

"Did you know Heather Ainsley?"

She pressed her lips together so hard they formed a thin white line. Twin spots of crimson rose on her cheekbones. Get more flies with honey? Fuck that. You got more flies by giving them shit, even if you were pulling it directly out of your own ass.

He leaned closer. "She's dead, too, Shandi. Just like Marius Brown. And if you think you're any safer than she was, either you're an idiot or a liar. Or both."

Her jaw dropped, eyes wide. "Fuck you," she hissed.

Shandi knew more than she was saying. Gene too. What the hell kind of hold did this fucker have over them? "I think you and Marius work for the same man, the man Heather Ainsley worked for. I need to know who he is." He watched her closely, but her lips were again pressed tightly together, chest rising and falling frantically—she was hyperventilating. She'd pass out if she wasn't careful.

*Who has you under their thumb, little girl?*

Shandi looked down, fists clenched. When she raised her head again, her breath had evened. "You've got this all wrong." But the voice wasn't hers, it was the drone of a robot —something she'd rehearsed? She gestured to the food bank around her. "I work here, not for some mystery person. And do any of us really look dangerous? Like people who'd hurt

Marius or Heather?" She dropped her hands and shook her head. "Of course not. It's our job to ease suffering."

*Our job is to ease suffering.* His stomach twisted. *My job is to ease suffering.* Oh shit. Those words…he knew where he'd heard them.

"If you remember anything about Marius…maybe give the precinct a call," he said slowly.

She nodded. "Of course." But she was lying about that, too; this girl knew more than she'd ever tell him, but he didn't need her. He already knew who their killer was. He just needed proof, and now he knew where he might get it.

## 19

THE STREETLIGHTS WHIZZED by on either side of the car, the lamps blurring into a single white line. The turn for the precinct appeared, approached—and passed. He'd call Mueller in a few hours, but he wasn't changing course now so someone else could step in and fuck this up. Hopefully, later he'd have something more solid than a hunch.

Why would anyone do things by the book? Impractical, that's what it was. But he still had to be careful; if he handled this wrong, Heather's killer would go free.

Petrosky parked down the road from St. Ignatius, and as he walked, the church emerged like a mirage in the sea of white, the stained glass windows glowing with flickering candlelight from the other side of the glass. The eastern sky was still black, though a line of purple—*not purple, indigo,* Heather's voice whispered—was visible at the edge of the horizon. It would be morning soon. And even at this hour, Father Norman would be somewhere in the building, waiting for one of his parishioners to seek him out, so he could offer words of wisdom and the gentle squeeze of a priestly hand meant to convey God's comfort.

But Father Norman was no god.

Father Norman was a man with a connection to the homeless shelter and its never-ending supply of vulnerable people. Father Norman accepted fistfuls of cash from men like Donald despite knowing they had barely enough to scrape by. He was a man whose job it was to ease suffering, by his own words, yet his most devout followers seemed to suffer more than most. Heather certainly had. And what better person for a desperate fifteen-year-old girl to cling to than the kindly priest? Heather wouldn't have been able to hide their engagement from him, either—might be why she hadn't wanted her father to know she was dating Petrosky. She had worried that Donald, with his twice-weekly confessions, would let it slip.

It might be a crazy idea. He was ready to be proven wrong. Hell, he *wanted* to be wrong—he didn't want this to be his fault. But who else did Heather know, who else did she really interact with? Her fellow volunteers said she rarely talked to anyone besides Gene. Yet no one would have thought twice about her communing with the priest.

*Like her mysterious benefactor would just show up out in the open.* But...

*My job is to ease suffering.*

He crept to the sidewalk, but instead of heading up the stone steps, he followed the path around the side of the church. Three stone birdbaths lined the right side of the walk that led to the back parking lot; to his left, a row of evergreen shrubs sat, crusted in snow and ice. No lights back here. Just the dark shadows, thick enough to choke on.

At the back corner of the church, he stepped off the shadowed path and into the lot, scanning the line of cars and trucks and vans the priest lent to those distributing goods, or for Sunday school field trips, or for the occasional parishioner who just needed help getting to work. Dark back there, too, but not so dark that he couldn't make out the colors of the vehicles. Nothing dark blue or black—the only truck back here was white, practically glowing in the hazy moonlight that reflected off the snow.

But that wasn't what drew his attention. He glanced back at the monster of a building behind him, half expecting to see a figure emerge from the shadows, gun raised, but the lot remained still. Silent. He turned back to the truck. Twenty feet away. Fifteen.

Over the rear wheel of the truck was a white bumper sticker, shining in the moonlight, stark black letters practically leaping from the sticker's surface: FOOD GIFTS. Down the row, a van bore the same sticker. The killer might have tried to peel it from his vehicle, but the pickup had probably come from this lot. And Father Norman could have walked to the appliance store from here yesterday morning—just stroll over, wait for Brown to come out, and shoot him in the chest. The man had experience in that regard; a soldier turned priest. That was one of the reasons Donald trusted him so implicitly—his service. His ability to wield a deadly weapon.

Fuck. *I should have thought about that before.*

Petrosky hurried back across the lot and ducked into the shadows along the side of the church, his jaw so tight he could hear his teeth grinding together. His nails bit into his palms. He climbed the stone steps.

*Keep it together. Patience.*

Petrosky took a deep breath and wrenched open the heavy oak door, and inside…

Silence. He headed for the confessionals, calling the priest's name, but Father Norman was not in the dim interior of the booths—not that he'd expected him to be in the hours before dawn. Petrosky dropped the confessional door and headed up the aisle, his footfalls echoing around him like the voice of God urging him to go home already. To let it go. To forget, to ignore, to shove it all down somewhere it wouldn't hurt, but despite the pain, despite his exhaustion, he felt more alive than he had in months.

*The fuck you want to be, boy?*

*I want to kill someone, sir.* Would that make the pain stop? It might. He wasn't sure he had the right man yet—but he would be.

The sound of his breath was sharp, the colors bolder than he remembered. Around him, his footsteps kept on as if they belonged to another, and his heart... Petrosky let the fire in his soul flame outward until his chest was burning, the edges of his vision dark, the tang of metal acidic in his throat.

Up and around the pulpit. Down the aisle to the back hallway again. Sweat trickled between his shoulder blades. The office doors were closed—locked. But Norman had to be there somewhere.

Maybe he was asleep, though Petrosky wasn't sure where the priest's living quarters were located.

So he'd make Norman come to him.

He headed back into the main church and crossed the aisle to the second row of pews, watching the giant suffering Christ above him. Endless pain. Fitting. If he was right about this, he'd give Father Norman endless pain, that miserable fuck. He inhaled deeply, and for a second, he swore he felt the dusty grit of sand in his nostrils.

Petrosky slid into the pew, knelt, and closed his eyes. He'd barely taken one breath when the image of Heather's bloody face smeared across his brain and made him want to open his lids once more, stare at the stained glass, the statues, the candles, anything to distract him from that gruesome visual. But he needed Norman to believe he was praying, and he didn't think people prayed with their eyes open. He clamped his eyelids shut. Heather's perfume clung to his sinuses. And there was her face the night she died, the hair he'd once pushed from her temple, and then her blood, covering his hands, the snow stained pink…sand in his nose, his friend blown to bits, the desert glare…Petrosky's fingers tingled, and he could feel the wetness, the slick mess sliding over his palms.

"Ed?"

His eyes snapped open, and he shot to his feet, woozy from the blood rushing to his head.

"No, no, Ed. No need to get up." Norman put a hand on his shoulder, and together they sat in the pew. Norman's eyes were soft, sad in the flickering candlelight, and the dark hollows beneath seemed to have lengthened since the day they'd picked up Heather's urn.

Guilt? Sorrow? A jealous man would have a soft spot for his…victim. Petrosky's back tightened, his skin burning where Norman had touched him, though he tried to keep his posture relaxed. The fucker was probably just worried about being caught.

"What brings you here, Ed?"

"I got some news on Heather's case. I needed a place to process it." The lie slipped out too easily.

"I see." Petrosky tried to meet the man's eyes, but Norman shook his head, dropping his gaze to the floor. "God's house is the right place for these worries."

"God's house and mine." When Norman's eyebrows went up, Petrosky finished: "The man who killed Heather had an accomplice, waiting in the truck the night Heather died—he put a bullet in my partner. That's why I'm here."

"You saw this person?"

The hairs on the back of his neck prickled. No, Petrosky hadn't—the man had been wearing a ski mask. And the way the priest's brow had relaxed told him Father Norman already knew that.

"I didn't see his face, but I believe I know who it was. Just trying to decide what to do about it."

Father Norman sat back in the pew, and Petrosky craned his neck to keep watch on the man. "I see," the priest said softly. "How can I help?" The bags under his eyes seemed to darken further still. And Norman's hands were definitely shaking.

"Nothing you can do, Father. I just thought you'd want to know."

Norman's hand rested on Petrosky's shoulder again, and he resisted the urge to shake it off. "I thank you, my son. And if there is any way I can help you now, perhaps take your confession…"

*Like I'm going into a dark booth with you.* Was that where the idea had gelled? The priest watching through the confessional's wooden lattice as Donald spilled his secrets, purging his pain at not being able to provide for his daughter? How long before Norman had propositioned Heather?

Petrosky had no idea. Because Norman was a keeper of secrets. All priests were.

"I just need to sit awhile—be in this place that Heather loved so much. Is that okay?"

Norman nodded, his gaze on his trembling hands. "Please stay as long as you'd like." Then he headed down the aisle toward the back hallway and vanished beyond the nave—walking faster than usual, Petrosky thought. *He's going to get a weapon.*

In the distance, a door opened, then closed again. Norman was in his office. Petrosky stood and stomped to the exit, but paused inside the enormous oak doors. He removed his shoes and tucked them under his arm, then pulled open the front door, hard, waiting to make sure the springs would catch it and pull it shut, before padding to the far back corner of the church, where the overhead lights did not reach. He slid beneath the back pew on his belly, crawling like he was in the sand, like he was back in the desert with Joey, inhaling gunpowder, listening to the rapid bursts of gunfire—he could almost taste the dirt in his teeth. The front door thunked closed, marking his supposed departure.

He wasn't sure what he was waiting for...but his gut told him to stay. To watch. The priest had told Petrosky, "stay as long as you'd like," which was consent to entry like a vampire who could only get you once you extended the invitation. Now he could take the bastard down based on whatever he saw here, and it would all be by the book—the fastest way to throw away your rights was to invite the cops inside. And if Norman thought Petrosky suspected him, he'd try to fix it, maybe make a call or two, and Petrosky could retrieve those numbers from the phone company later. If Norman left, Petrosky would follow. If he met with someone, called some young girl to quell his agitation, to relieve his stress, Petrosky would see it. Or Norman would call in reinforcements, another accomplice like Brown, to go after Petrosky himself. What better place than these hallowed halls to hatch a murder plot?

Minutes passed, though Petrosky wasn't certain how many. His ribs ached from pressing against the wooden floor. A stale draft whooshed past his face. He let his body sink into the moment, his eyes open to the dust mites, and listened, hoping for the sound of footsteps approaching from somewhere else in the building, but the silence wrapped itself around him like a cloak, only the wind against the rafters testing the limits of the silent, hazy dimness that had settled in his bones.

The wood pressed harder against his belly. He stared up the row toward the aisle, concentrating on...the blankness. *Blank.* The ache in his lower back intensified, then eased. *Blank.* His chin cooled against the wood. *Blank. Blank. Blank.*

He had just closed his eyes when a distant rumbling made him raise his head off the floor. He strained his ears, but the sound did not repeat. Had he imagined it?

No, there was another noise—a *thup* like a car door slamming, and though the snow should have swallowed up the sound, it cracked like a small explosion through the building.

*Scree.* The front door squealed open, then thunked closed again. Petrosky's line of sight was blocked by the pillars on either side of the aisle—he had to wait until the newcomer stepped farther into the church before he'd be able to see their feet moving down the line of pews. From the back hallway came another *thunk*—Father Norman's office door— then the sound of the priest's shoes *click-clicking* down the aisle. Norman paused as if surprised to see his guest. Then he started down the aisle once more.

Petrosky's muscles tensed. *Wait. Listen.* He had to catch Norman in the act—needed to hear them say something incriminating. Even then, it'd be his word against the priest's.

Then the person by the door moved, stepping hesitantly past the pillars and into Petrosky's line of vision: Shandi's tiny green sneakers, her tentative steps the rubber-on-wood equivalent of crying. But the priest clacked up the aisle with the hard, quick, purposeful gait of someone on a mission. Closer, closer, past Shandi, out of Petrosky's sight. *Oh shit.* Did Norman suspect he was hiding down here? Was the priest coming now to shoot him in the back of the skull? But then Petrosky heard a *clunk*—the deadbolt on the front doors. Norman had locked them in.

More footsteps. Petrosky's hackles rose, his fists clenched, but the priest wasn't coming toward him— Norman was heading to the opposite end of the nave where the confessional booths sat. Another door creaked, so sudden and obnoxious that Petrosky winced, and the confessional door slammed shut.

*Listen to yer gut*, Patrick would say. *That Norman is a rumbly bloke.* A dodgy fellow.

And Petrosky's gut said that girl wasn't here to confess shit. He might be just a flatfoot, but he wasn't an idiot.

Petrosky pushed himself from the space beneath the pew and stepped back into the shadows, scanning the church for any other signs of life. He saw only the gentle flicker of the candles. A barely-there murmur drifted from the opposite side of the room.

Petrosky slunk to the confessional door, the whisper of his socks on the wood as unnerving as the *shh shh* slithering of a snake. But there'd be no forbidden trees or ill-gotten apples today. Only justice. The door of the confessional booth was cool to the touch. He put his ear to the wood, and the muffled sound of sobbing trickled through.

"I'm afraid he knows." Shandi. Was Norman using her too? Paying her for...what? Sexual favors? That's why Heather hadn't denied being a prostitute; she'd sure felt like one.

"What makes you think he knows?" Norman asked.

"He was there, at the warehouse, and—"

"My child, what I asked you to do might not have been orthodox, but there is nothing to be ashamed of."

*Nothing to be ashamed of?* Norman was going to get a fist through his jawbone if he tried to sell prostitution or drugs or murder as "a little unorthodox."

"But he knows about Heather!"

"You have no secrets, my child."

If Norman had ordered Heather's execution and murdered Marius Brown, he had more than secrets to worry about.

Shandi's voice devolved into desperate sobbing. "I just...I still don't even know why I was supposed to watch her! And now she's dead, she's... I can't..." She was wheezing now, gasping.

Petrosky squinted. *Wait, what? Watch her?* If Norman had told Shandi to stalk Heather, to notify him when she'd be alone, then Shandi was an accomplice. No wonder she hadn't wanted to tell him anything.

"I know, my child. Grief is a terrible—"

"Do you know who hurt her? Will they hurt me?"

"My child, you know I cannot—"

"The hell you can't!" A bang came from inside the confessional as if she'd slammed her fist against the wooden bench. "You knew she was in trouble—that's why you wanted me to watch her!"

Was that true? No, Norman had wanted Shandi to watch Heather so he could go after her.

"I...I just don't know what to do," she whispered. A shuffle, like she was standing, and Petrosky stepped back, looking for a place to hide. Ten steps to the pews, but he'd never make it to the back in time. Only five steps to the hallway.

He booked it for Norman's office, waiting for the creaking and slamming of the confessional door, for Norman to call his name, for the *clackity clack* of footsteps giving chase, but no noise came from the nave as he ducked into the hallway and took the dozen steps toward the offices. He stopped at the door beside Norman's—locked. But the crack beneath the door of Father Norman's office glowed with lamplight.

*Click.* The door opened. Petrosky paused at the threshold, again listening for movement from the front of the church, but Norman had apparently convinced Shandi to stay—and he wouldn't kill her here. He was too smart for that. He knew how to ensure nothing incriminated him. That's why he'd hired Brown—and created the infamous Otis Messinger.

And a few whispered words from a girl who clearly didn't

know her boss's dark secrets wasn't enough to charge Norman with murder. Petrosky needed more. He wanted this bastard to go away forever…if he didn't take the guy out himself first. Behind the desk, the window smoldered, the glass subtly orange with impending dawn.

Petrosky stuck his head out the door and listened, and when no noise came from the church, he eased the door closed and ran for the top desk drawer, dropping his shoes. Pencils and coins, mostly—he pushed aside a rosary, lifted a pad of sticky notes. The second drawer contained more of the same. He turned from the desk to the two-drawer filing cabinet in the back corner of the room and squatted in front of it—locked. The Swiss Army knife he'd lifted from the precinct's file-room clerk made short work of the latch. Thank goodness he'd kept it—thing was coming in handy.

He yanked open the bottom drawer, and a bright *clink* rang through the air. Petrosky paused, listening for anyone who might catch him, and when all remained silent, he peeked inside and found a half-empty bottle of cheap gin jammed beside a short stack of hanging files. He pulled out the bottle along with the files and flipped through the folders. Lists of volunteers. Bible verses, half-written sermons. Old calendars with the dates of baptisms and funerals.

Petrosky shifted back on his heels and froze there, gaze locked on the desk. The opening for the chair was normal, but the sides where the drawers went seemed…wrong. He squinted. Yes, the drawers on one side reached lower than the other, as if the bottom desk drawer on the right side was deeper. Surely the desk hadn't come that way. And as he crawled toward it, he could make out a tiny crevice, about where the drawer should end, with the wood beneath a slightly different shade than the drawer above. He ran his fingers along the side of the drawer—smooth until he reached the crevice. Someone had glued a box under the desk. He reached below—

*There.*

A tiny half-moon cutout on the bottom. He stuck his finger inside and pulled, and a thin panel of wood slid back, a gentle *thump* cutting the frantic hiss of his breath—something had fallen out. A checkbook lay open on the carpet, two names on the account: Heather Ainsley and Otis Messinger. And now the bubble letters Heather had doodled on the back of her files at home made even more sense. Big Daddy. Who better to be "Big Daddy" than *Father* Norman?

"Goddammit. You motherfucking—"

"I'll ask you not to take the Lord's name in vain here, my son."

Petrosky jolted upright, narrowly missing the desktop with his forehead as he shot to his feet, fumbling his gun from his holster and taking aim.

Norman stood in the doorway with the girl in front of him like a human shield, his hands on Shandi's thin shoulders, her body trembling, her eyes cast down toward her tiny green sneakers.

## 20

Norman was a blank slate, but as the girl raised her head, her face was all too easy to read: Shandi was terrified. Petrosky narrowed his eyes. Norman appeared unarmed, but that didn't mean the guy couldn't snap her bird neck with one move, as some of Petrosky's comrades had done during the war.

"Lower the gun, Ed."

Petrosky's right eye twitched. The girl began to cry.

"Let her go, Norman."

Norman's eyes widened. "She's here of her own free will." He raised his hands, but Shandi stayed where she was, backing up until her shoulders were against the priest's chest.

"Are you going to kill us?" she whispered, her voice shaking. "Please don't kill us."

Petrosky kept the gun aimed at Norman's face, but his mind was racing. *This girl is afraid of...me?*

*It's a trap.*

*He'll kill you as soon as you let your guard down.*

But that girl's face, streaked with tears... Norman didn't

have a weapon, and there were no pockets that Petrosky could see in the priest's tunic. He lowered his gun but kept his finger on the trigger.

"It appears we need to have a talk, Ed." The priest's voice was mellow as ever, but now Petrosky could hear the manipulative timbre there, the kind of voice practiced to encourage placidity in those around you. So you could control them.

He tightened his grip on the weapon.

"Shandi, you go on out," Norman said softly. "This is just a conversation between friends."

Petrosky almost said, "You're not in charge here, Norman," but he didn't want Shandi there any more than Norman did.

The girl hesitated, staring at him, then Norman.

"Go," Petrosky said.

She scrambled for the hall, leaving the door open behind her. Norman turned his back on Petrosky and closed it, and when he faced Petrosky again, his eyes were drawn—watery.

*Faker. You're going to tell me you killed her, you asshole.*

Norman sat in the chair in front of the desk, and Petrosky took the seat across from him, aiming the gun at Norman underneath the desktop in case the man had some hidden artillery he wasn't privy to.

"Let's hear it, Norman."

"Father Norman."

"Some fucking priest you are."

Norman frowned but did not respond.

"Tell me about this." Petrosky tossed the checkbook into the man's lap. Norman didn't even bother to glance at it, just kept his eyes locked on Petrosky's.

"It's a joint checking account."

"I know that, genius. How about you tell me why you were paying Heather." *Tell me what you did to her, you fucking tell me.*

"I wasn't paying her. I was…supporting her."

"Right," Petrosky said, staring daggers at Norman. How had Heather ever trusted this guy? But…he had too. Petrosky cleared his throat. "Did you kill her because you didn't want anyone to find out how you made her earn that support?"

"I didn't kill her."

"Sure you didn't." His shoulders screamed with tension. The air around them had thinned, as if Norman had replaced all the oxygen in the room with bullshit. "That girl who just left…you paying her for kinky stuff too?"

"You're welcome to talk to Shandi. Ask her whatever you wish."

*She won't tell me shit.* "Why don't you explain why she's here now. I'm sure cooperation will go a long way with the district attorney."

Norman's lips quivered, but he clamped his mouth shut and said nothing. Then, in a voice so soft it was almost imperceptible: "She was looking after Heather for me."

*I don't even know why I was supposed to watch her!*

"And why would you have been watching Heather?" The priest's lip was still trembling—scared. Guilty as sin. "It's almost as if you needed someone to keep tabs on her, someone to make sure she showed up behind that school so you could murder her in cold blood."

"I did no such thing. But I do have people I trust, people who looked in on her from time to time. She was quiet, shy, as you know." And on the word "shy," his voice cracked, though not with the pain of grief—this was hotter, sharper, some ill-concealed rage Petrosky could not place.

"People you trust…so more people than just Shandi? Gene too?" *Used to call here all the time, had a thing for her.*

Norman swallowed hard, then nodded slowly.

He'd had an army out there, watching Heather. But he

had no reason to follow her unless he knew she was in trouble.

"I just wanted to keep her safe."

"So you knew she was in danger." *Because you put her in danger, you sorry motherfucker.*

"I only suspected. I even paged her that day to warn her, to tell her to be careful."

"You were the one who paged—"

He held up a hand. "I never thought it'd go so far; that it would happen this…way." His breath hitched again, but this time, his eyes filled. "I thought I'd get to marry the two of you at my altar, watch her walk down the aisle, that I'd baptize your children." Tears overflowed, trailing down his cheeks, and Petrosky's hand slackened around his gun. Was Norman that good a liar, just faking it? Or were those tears of guilt?

"Well, if it wasn't you, *Father*, who was it? Who killed her?"

The priest looked beyond Petrosky, the orange glow of sunrise glinting in his irises like flames.

Petrosky raised one fist and slammed it into the desktop so hard that Norman jumped. "Stop fucking me around and tell me what you know."

"I'm afraid I can't do that, my son." Norman crossed his arms, and now his eyes were cold, steely—determined. "Some things aren't meant to see daylight."

"You're not going to pull some confessional privilege bullshit—"

"It's not bull, as you say. I am only a conduit. Confession is a sacred bond between the Lord and his children."

"If someone confessed to killing Heather—"

"They didn't."

"Then how the fuck—"

"Past transgressions are often singular in nature—a

mistake, a momentary lapse in judgment. But sometimes they repeat. If we see the signs, we intervene where we can; the rest we leave to God."

"Your God got my fiancée killed, so you'll have to excuse me if I don't buy into that shit—"

"The Lord works in ways we don't always understand."

"That's where we differ, Norman: I need to understand. And I won't stop until I do."

"He'll kill you."

"Come again?"

Norman's lips slammed shut, and he inhaled deeply through his nostrils, then let it out so slowly Petrosky wanted to punch him right in the schnoz. "The fear of the Lord prolongs life, but the years of the wicked will be shortened."

"That wasn't what you were going to say." *Fear of the Lord, my ass—God has nothing to do with this.* "And if you think your God wants to kill me for looking into Heather's death, you're not making a case for religious people being sane." He leaned over the desk, staring into Norman's eyes. "Let's pretend I believe you. If you took confession from someone dangerous, a killer, it's only a matter of time before they do it again. You're putting your entire congregation at risk."

"The risk has passed."

"From your statement a moment ago, it sounds like you think I might be on the short list."

"Beware of false prophets," the priest blurted out, "who come to you in sheep's clothing but inwardly are ravenous wolves." He wiped his eyes. "Matthew 7:15."

"Don't fuck with someone who has a gun pointed at you." Petrosky raised the barrel above the desktop and leveled it at Norman. "Courtesy of some hooker I met over on the east side. A wise woman."

"The risk will be over soon," Norman repeated, and

something in his face reminded Petrosky of Heather, the way she looked at the end of a long a day—exhausted but relieved.

"You can't be sure there's no more risk. But you can be sure you'll spend time in a jail cell if you don't start talking."

"My bond with the Lord will see me through all challenges so long as I keep my faith."

About this, Petrosky believed him. He could lock Norman up tomorrow, and the guy would sit there, lips sealed, for eternity.

But none of this explained why he'd be giving Heather money. "You said you were supporting her, but you can't support every member of your congregation. So why Heather?"

"Heather was special."

"The way Marius Brown was special?"

The priest's eyes narrowed.

"Marius came into a lot of money just after Heather died. I assume that was you, paying him to kill her with the cash from Heather's accounts?" *Admit it, you fuck.* But the certainty he'd had when he'd arrived had mellowed into a heavy unease in the pit of his stomach.

The priest's nostrils flared. Petrosky's uncertainty vanished—no one had access to those secret accounts but Father Norman. Why else would he keep them behind a hidden panel under his desk? And despite how obvious it was, the guy still couldn't admit it.

"Jesus Christ, stop fucking around and tell me the goddamn truth! If you didn't kill her yourself, you knew enough to stop it. And you sure as shit know how Marius Brown was connected to it."

"Marius helped me look out for Heather, I won't deny it."

"And she just happened to die on his watch, with him

covered in her blood, right before you paid him off." Petrosky tapped the butt of his gun on the wood.

Norman's jaw clenched. "Yes, I gave the money to Marius. Heather didn't need it any longer."

*I fucking knew it.* "But Donald needs it. That's why she was saving it. And that money was there until you paid Marius Brown to kill her."

"I did no such thing." But his face had hardened, and his eyes were cloudy—less determined. Was that fear?

"Then why pay him?"

"You'll have to ask him."

*Ask him.* Present tense. "We found Marius Brown's body today," Petrosky said slowly, examining the priest's face. "Shot to death."

Norman's jaw dropped. His skin paled—shock. *He didn't know.* Then: "No. No, it can't…Marius? He was troubled, but…oh, no." The dam broke. His shoulders trembled. Tears streamed down his cheeks. No way the priest was that good a liar.

"Why would someone kill Marius, Father?"

"I can't answer that." Norman stared again through the window into the daybreak. His face was wet. "It's time for you to go." He watched the rising sun as Petrosky shoved the gun into its holster and grabbed his shoes. The checkbook lay open in Norman's lap—Petrosky snatched that up too.

"Ed?"

He turned back at the door to see Norman's gaze locked on him, his face earnest. "Be wise as serpents and innocent as doves."

Innocent as doves. Like the ones Heather would never get to breed.

**21**

———

Petrosky headed for the station, expecting Mueller or Patrick to be waiting in the morning sunlight, ready to arrest him for pulling a weapon on Father Norman. But no one looked up as he strode through the bullpen toward Mueller's desk. The detective was already on his feet.

"You seen Patrick?" Petrosky asked.

"Lost your partner, eh? He'll turn up."

*Should I tell him?* But what would Petrosky say? That Father Norman had said *someone* in his church had killed Heather? That he'd been aiming a gun at the priest's face the whole time?

"Anything new on the Marius Brown case?"

"Just the autopsy." Mueller shrugged into his coat. "Single gunshot wound, downward trajectory; looks like someone was sitting on top of the building next door, waiting for him to walk out. He probably never saw it coming."

Sniped him from the roof—the killer hadn't even gotten his hands dirty.

Mueller turned toward the stairs, and Petrosky put a hand on his shoulder. "Hey, Mueller, can you wait a—"

137

"I have to run. Next of kin notification on Brown, took forever to find her. Mother got married and never bothered to change her name with the state or the DMV, just moved in with her hubby. Let her driver's license lapse and everything." Mueller frowned at Petrosky's hand, and Petrosky dropped his arm. "I fucking hate these," Mueller muttered.

"Can I ride along?" While Norman had admitted to giving Brown the money, they needed to prove it had been more than charity. Maybe Marius Brown's family had insight into Brown's sudden influx of cash…and what Brown might have been willing to do for it. Because even if Norman hadn't paid Brown to kill Heather—and Petrosky still wasn't entirely certain he believed it—you didn't give someone that kind of money unless they'd earned it.

---

"CAN you think of a reason anyone would want to hurt your son?"

Grace Johnson shook her head, her shoulders slumped—defeated. "He was…troubled, so I can't know for certain. Into drugs and the like. Never could seem to get it together."

Troubled—the same word Father Norman had used, almost like the two of them had discussed it beforehand.

"I told him to come back when he got clean, thought tough love was the way to do it…" She wiped tears from her cheeks. "After I cut him off, he spent most of his time over at that shelter."

Cut him off, huh? Was that the reason Brown had kept going to work despite all that cash in the bank? Because he couldn't get to the money?

Mueller pressed on: "We have reason to believe your son might have killed a woman a few months before his death."

Her eyes widened. "Marius? Not my Marius."

Ah, love. When you're too close to see a person for what they really are.

"We have a positive ID. A witness. An influx of money into his bank account the day after the murder."

She stared at the wall behind them, her knuckles white. The silence stretched.

"Did you know Heather Ainsley?"

Her jaw tightened, but she drew her gaze back to Mueller's face.

"Ma'am?"

Now she looked down. "I knew her mother." Her voice was tight, but not with sadness this time—she sounded pissed.

"Your son was at the scene of Ainsley's murder," Mueller said. "Covered in her blood. We believe he killed her, but what we can't figure out is why."

If he'd killed her for the money, there didn't need to be another reason. But this woman had cut her son off. When? Had she been controlling Brown's accounts at the time of Heather's death? And if that were the case...why would Brown have bothered earning it by killing Heather in the first place?

Her jaw clenched, released, clenched, released.

"Ma'am?" Mueller said again.

She clamped her lips tighter together.

"How did you cut him off?" Petrosky asked. "Didn't he have his own bank accounts?"

"I... They're mine. He didn't know about them—I just put them in his name. I thought once he was better..."

*She's the one Norman was paying?*

Petrosky and Mueller exchanged a glance. *Come on, lady, give me something.* He needed a reason to know about Father

Norman's involvement besides breaking into the priest's desk or stalking the homeless shelter, where he absolutely was not supposed to have been.

"If Marius spent time at the homeless shelter, do you think he was close to anyone there? Maybe made friends at the church up the road?" Petrosky stared at her, level, unflinching. Her nostrils flared.

"I know a lot of those boys go down to see Father Norman, and if someone out there had it in for Marius…" He glanced at Mueller again. "Maybe we should ask the priest."

Her face changed almost imperceptibly, panic glittering through her grief. Mueller stiffened—he must have seen it too.

She stared at Petrosky as if assessing her options, then dropped her chin to her chest. "I knew this would happen eventually."

Mueller balked. "You knew Marius would murder—"

"No, people…finding out…" She sighed.

"Finding out what?" Mueller asked, but Petrosky's world had slowed.

"Well, me and…I mean, you know. That's why you're here, right? Because he gave Marius Heather's money?"

"Ma'am—"

"I didn't want to get him in trouble, okay? I thought about it sometimes—I hated that Marius went to church there, that they had any contact at all. But he paid child support so long as I didn't tell anyone he was Marius's father—I don't even think Marius knew."

Mueller squinted. "Marius's father? Who are we—"

"Father Norman," Petrosky said. Mueller jerked his head in Petrosky's direction, then back to Grace as she nodded.

"Does Father Norman know?" Mueller asked. "About Marius's death?"

*Yes.*

"Well, I sure didn't tell him—I haven't seen him in years." She shrugged. "We didn't leave things on good terms."

Mueller leaned closer. "And why is that, ma'am?"

She wiped her eyes. "I was far from the only one."

# 22

"THE GODDAMN PRIEST. Can you believe that?" Mueller tapped his fingers on the steering wheel. "You've got some good instincts, Petrosky."

But the words seeped toward him as through a fog. He'd had it all wrong. Father Norman was Marius Brown's father, Heather's father, paying his children to keep their paternity a secret. Brown hadn't needed "Otis Messinger"—his mother had set up the account for him. But Heather had needed a co-signer; when the priest began paying her, she was fifteen, and Donald must not have known that Heather wasn't his. Otherwise, she wouldn't have made up that elaborate story about bookkeeping, and Donald sure wouldn't have been friendly with Norman if he knew the priest had slept with his wife. Why Norman had waited until she was a teenager to pay out, Petrosky had no idea—maybe Heather's mother hadn't wanted to raise red flags by having extra cash around. But once Nancy committed suicide, and Norman realized Heather needed the funds...

Still, why had Heather been walking the street the night they met if she had all that cash? Why had both she and

Marius Brown been murdered? Though…it was possible that someone was targeting the priest because of his affairs. He sighed. Why the hell did Norman get to ignore the whole celibacy thing but keep confessional secrets? That was some religious cherry-picking right there.

"I'll drop you off at the station," Mueller was saying. "I want to spend some time over at the church today, chat with this Father Norman and see what I can dig up." He shook his head. "The motherfucking priest."

But Petrosky already knew what Norman would tell Mueller: a whole lot of jack. Hopefully, he'd leave out the part about Petrosky's early morning visit. He stared out the window at the melting snow. "Be wise as serpents and innocent as doves. Have fun with that."

"Behold, I send you out as sheep in the midst of wolves," Mueller said with a snort. "I never pegged you for a religious man."

Petrosky turned from the window. "What?"

"The rest of that quote. 'Behold, I send you out as sheep in the midst of wolves, so be wise as serpents and innocent as doves.' My grandmother used to say that all the time."

In the midst of wolves. A wolf in sheep's clothing… What else had Norman said? Something about false prophets that looked like sheep but were…ravenous wolves. *Wolves, wolves.* That was a little coincidental. So, what was Norman trying to tell him? No one had confessed to Heather's murder if he believed the priest…but maybe Norman had a guess about who'd killed Marius Brown.

Wolves. The *lone wolf.*

*No.* That wasn't possible. It made no sense at all.

*Father Norman is fucking with me.*

But what if he wasn't?

*The fear of the Lord prolongs life, but the years of the wicked will be shortened.*

A short life—someone sick. Dying.

"You okay?" Mueller asked.

"Yeah, I'm fine," Petrosky said, trying to keep his voice even. "Just have a few things to take care of back at the precinct."

"No worries. I'll drop you off so you can find your partner."

But he wasn't doing this with a partner.

*The fuck you want to be, boy?*

*Certain, sir.*

Certain.

**23**

———

DONALD SAT STARING out the front window, eyes dull, trembling hands resting on the dog in his lap. "What do you need, Ed? I'm awfully tired." He looked it, too—pale skin, gaunt cheeks, sunken rib cage.

*I have to be wrong about this.* But if someone had killed Petrosky's daughter...

"Listen, Donald, Marius Brown, the man who murdered Heather...he was found dead yesterday. Shot, downward trajectory like from a sniper rifle."

"Huh."

"Did you know him, Donald?" Petrosky's muscles were coiled so tightly he feared they might snap. Donald's gaze remained locked on the window. "The shelter is right up the road from the church; maybe Marius went over there sometimes? Maybe you met him at bingo night?"

"Not sure."

"Donald...I need you to level with me," he said, and the old man finally turned to face Petrosky, eyes shining now. "If I go into the attic for your old rifle, am I going to find it's been recently fired? Will they be able to match your gun to the bullet we pulled out of Marius's chest?"

The man blinked, his pale face ghostlike in the beams of sunlight from the window. "Just how do you think I got over there to do this thing? Look at me, son." He gestured to his legs—thin, but...not as atrophied as they should be. "You think I miraculously shed this chair every evening?"

The stop Petrosky had made on his way here suggested exactly that. "I think you do—or at least you can."

"But—"

"Your social worker told me you had physical therapy, but that she didn't worry about it when the check bounced because you didn't need PT anymore—even though you still weren't walking."

"It wasn't helping."

"Maybe not. The physical therapist said you could walk just fine—your muscles were working even though you refused to get up." Petrosky followed Donald's gaze to the dog in his lap, one of Roscoe's tiny feet splayed on top of the wheelchair's arm. "I don't understand why you'd pretend to be worse off than you are."

"I have a lot to atone for, Ed—you were a military man, you understand."

"I understand the guilt,"—*god, did he*—"but why the chair?"

"This is my penance."

"How would sitting in a wheelchair undo whatever you did in the war? Even if you crippled someone else—"

"Some things need to be done for the sake of the soul." Donald's jaw quivered, and he lowered his voice to a whisper. "And Marius deserved what he got."

*Jesus Christ, he did do it.* The man had somehow made it three miles to the appliance store, climbed to the roof of the adjacent building, waited until Brown walked out, and put a bullet in his heart? Had someone else driven him, or had he carried this out all on his own? What the fuck was happening here? Donald opened his mouth again as if to speak, but Petrosky put up his palm—*stop*. "Don't say anything else without a lawyer." If Brown had killed Petrosky's daughter, he'd have shot him too—shit, he'd have crawled on his hands and knees up three flights of stairs to make it happen. Maybe Petrosky wouldn't say anything to the police at all, just let the old man die in peace. Donald wouldn't even make it to the end of the trial before he kicked off.

Petrosky ran a hand over his unshaven face, feeling ten years older, and followed Donald's gaze to the crucifix. Jesus stared accusingly as if Petrosky himself had nailed him to the wood. Marius had killed Heather, drug deal, maybe, or just craziness. And Donald had killed the man who murdered his daughter. But something else was bothering Petrosky. "How did you know Marius killed Heather?" The police hadn't figured it out until yesterday, and that was only because Petrosky had given them an ID—they definitely hadn't made it public yet.

"Lucky guess."

"You killed a man on a guess?" Did Donald have an inside track at the precinct? The hairs on his neck stood on end.

"I asked him at bingo—you were right about that. And he admitted it."

That didn't ring true—*How would he know to ask Marius in the first place?*—but it was possible. "Do you know who the other man in the car was? The man who shot my partner?" Donald might have killed Marius after the fact, but he hadn't sat there and watched Marius murder his only child.

Donald shook his head. Petrosky's gaze dropped to the box on the table, Donald's medal surrounded by walls of glass along with a framed snapshot: Donald kneeling, a sniper's rifle on his shoulder after his last solo mission.

The lone wolf.

Donald saw him looking and sniffed once, hard. "I'm not sorry, Ed. Marius—"

"You need to call a lawyer, Don."

"Now that boy's soul has a chance of going to Heaven. You know it's easier to get in if someone else takes you out. Your sins are forgiven—it's automatic."

Petrosky drew his gaze from the glass box, the colors around him fading to gray. That sure didn't sound like any sermon he'd ever heard. "You think Marius gets into Heaven now because you killed him? After he murdered your daughter?"

Donald's eyes were still locked on his medal. "We talked about this in the jungle all the time. How we were helping those bastards, easing their eternal suffering—we were heroes."

Petrosky wouldn't justify what he'd done during the war. He couldn't. But Donald had needed a reason for each life he took, an excuse—so he'd created one: *For the sake of the soul.*

For the sake of the soul… The room heated as something critical snapped into place inside Petrosky's brain. Norman had said he hadn't heard a confession on Heather's murder; he'd heard another confession, something huge, something dangerous. Petrosky had thought Norman was talking about Marius Brown's murder, but no—Norman had been shocked. The priest hadn't known Brown was dead until Petrosky told him.

The room spun, the sunlight suddenly so bright he could scarcely make out the details of Donald's face, just the silhouette of an old man still staring at the box on the table, at the picture of the gun that had made him a "hero." If this was connected to Heather, to Donald, if this secret Norman knew was the reason the priest was keeping tabs on her…had Norman been watching Heather because he knew Donald was unstable? With all this soul bullshit, that would make sense. But Norman had said something about past transgressions being "singular," just a mistake. That didn't fit with what Donald had done in the jungle. Had Donald hurt someone else? If he'd known about his wife and the priest, though...

In Donald's world, infidelity was most certainly a sin.

The story was that Nancy had waited until Heather had gone to school, then lay in bed and put one of Donald's handguns to her temple. But what if she hadn't been the one who pulled the trigger?

"Did you kill your wife, Donald?" *For the sake of her soul?*

Donald's gaze had hardened. He stared, unblinking, but he did not deny it. Heat blossomed in Petrosky's chest and raced down his arms to his hands, tightening his fists.

*For the sake of the soul.* The line ran around and around in his mind—what had Donald said after they picked up Heather's ashes? That Heather hadn't done what she should have for the sake of her soul, that he'd...done all he could for her. "Did you...did you kill Heather too?" His voice shook. "Ease her suffering by giving her your Oxy pills before you shattered her skull?" But why? What monstrous sin did Donald think Heather had committed?

Donald's hands clenched in his lap, and the tiny dog jumped to his feet yelping, but Donald snatched the pup's leg before he could leap to the floor. The dog whined, frantically licking Donald's fingers as if his love could make the man release him. But this man knew nothing about love. And Donald's hands no longer trembled—not at all.

*He killed her.* Why the fuck had he killed her? "You let Heather stick around as long as she took care of you, as long as your bills were paid, but when you found out she was going to leave you"—*for me*—"you decided to—"

"I don't care about the money. I'll be dead and buried before the foreclosure's final," Donald spat. "I spent all my life trying to do right. I atoned, I confessed, I gave my money to the church. But God kept throwing things at me. First, it was my wife messing around on me with that…that…*false prophet.*"

He'd known from the beginning, known about the priest, about the money. And after they moved, he'd told Heather he was sick, sat down in that wheelchair, and he'd never gotten up again. Even Father Norman thought he was ill; that's why he wasn't turning Donald in now. He thought the man was dying and no longer a risk—just a sheep. But Donald had always been a wolf. "Were you ever sick?"

"The mind can be as riddled as the body." He looked down. "But yes, I am sicker now—cancer, not that I'm treating it. Back then, I got into that chair to show Heather what it was to humble yourself. Her mother got knocked up talking to people she shouldn't—if she hadn't spoken to the other fornicators, maybe she'd have stayed on a righteous path. Silence should have saved Heather from the sins of her mother and kept her out of trouble. Silence should have been Heather's penance—keeping silent is a virtue."

*Silence?* No wonder Heather had been so good at keeping secrets, why she'd been so wary of talking to anyone. And she'd probably known, or at least suspected, that Donald could walk, too—she'd been awfully confident that he could live on his own. "You took your own motion by sitting in that chair, and took Heather's voice by…what? Beating her when she talked too much?" Or maybe she'd feared Donald would kill her like he'd killed her mother. Had she known?

"God likes obedience."

Petrosky's blood boiled. This wasn't about obedience, this was about manipulation—secrets. And Heather hadn't kept silent. Heather *had* talked to Petrosky. But she hadn't told him everything. If she had, he could have protected her.

"No matter what I did, I couldn't save her from her nature." The dull cast in Donald's gaze brightened to something that wasn't quite fury, wasn't quite guilt—some stifled emotion locked deep beneath the lies he told himself. And Petrosky had suspected everyone except the man in front of him. Guilt and grief mingled with the hatred in his chest. Next time, he'd make sure to put that blame where it fucking belonged.

"Tell me what you did to her." *Say it, you piece of shit.* Had he paid Brown to kill her? Had Brown only been the driver? Petrosky wanted—*needed*—to hear every detail, to feel the wounds as if they were his own; he owed Heather that much before he turned it off forever.

Donald shook his head. "You don't understand. You're blind, like that *Marius*." He sniffed. "Always following her around, putting his nose where it didn't belong."

Following… Finally, the pieces fell into place. Brown had followed Heather that night because he'd been watching her for Father Norman. Petrosky saw Brown's dull eyes, his bloody hands moving in slow motion, the shock. Brown hadn't killed her, he'd *found* her. Her broken ribs weren't because someone had stomped her, but because Brown had tried to revive her. He'd tried to perform CPR. And when Brown had returned to the pickup, he'd found a masked killer waiting for him with a gun pointed at his head. But still…

"Why not kill Marius the night Heather died?"

"I thought he might repent."

"But why didn't he turn you in?"

A smile touched Donald's lips, just the tiniest of smirks, but horrific madness lay deep beneath it.

"He didn't know who I was." *The mask.* "And I told him I'd kill his mother."

"Would you have killed her?"

He shrugged. "Fornicators deserve what they get—she has hope of salvation, but not on her own."

"Yeah, when I hear 'salvation,' the first thing that comes to mind is always bludgeoning someone with a fucking crowbar."

"Heather had a chance at salvation even with her whore of a mother," he snarled. "But she betrayed me too, going to see that fornicator, volunteering where the false prophet told her to, then leaving me here in my last days to live with... you." He leaned closer, eyes wild.

*She's a good girl, a good, good girl.* "What the hell is wrong with you?"

"Do you think you could have saved her soul, Edward? Could you have saved her from the two-faced tramp she'd become? I couldn't die knowing that you didn't have it in you to make that sacrifice. You didn't see her sneaking out of the house dressed like a whore—she may have only done it once, but she never repented, never once begged for forgiveness. She was destined to be a Jezebel, just like her mother."

Snuck out once...once. Because she'd had a date with Gene. And she'd been so terrified of her father finding out, that she'd let Petrosky believe she was a hooker—wasn't that worse? But she hadn't admitted it, just never denied it... never said anything at all, not until he'd already taken off the cuffs. Maybe she'd just been frozen with fear when Petrosky picked her up, too terrified to correct him, scared her father would find out she'd even been *suspected* of streetwalking— not like Donald would believe the daughter of a whore.

No wonder Heather hadn't told Donald about them until Petrosky showed up unannounced—why when he'd let it slip that they were dating, she'd moved out, though they'd never even talked about living together. Why she insisted they go out in public with Donald instead of visiting him at home. *One more reason to get out of the house and enjoy each day,* she whispered in his head. She'd been scared of Donald, but she had thought her father was dying. She'd never realized he planned to take her with him.

Roscoe whimpered, and Petrosky put his hand on the butt of his gun. *I should shoot this fucker right now.* No, he should call for backup. "I suppose you think you can save me too." Petrosky stepped closer, staring into Donald's shining eyes. Not a twitch. Not a tremble.

"You got the wheelchair, you told Heather to close her mouth...what do I need, Donald?"

"Only took a few minutes to find out."

"Did you break into my house, Donald?"

The man said nothing. Then: "Those eyes are your burden, always looking at things you don't need to see." He lowered his voice to a whisper as if confiding some juicy secret, and maybe he thought he was. "Heather's notebooks, her thoughts laid bare like that...she could have written anything about me. *Anything.* I couldn't find them all, but when they surface, when you read them, you'll be just as damned."

Right, damned. This asshole just wanted to know if she'd written anything incriminating about him. "So I should take out my eyes, then? Because the mere prospect of seeing her words is such a terrible sin?"

"Only if you want salvation."

The man was out of his fucking mind. Maybe he'd gone to the jungle normal, but he'd come back a maniac.

*The fuck you want to be, boy?*

*Sane, sir. Not like this asshole.*

"Heather didn't need saving," Petrosky growled. "You sacrificed your child on the altar of your own insecurity and some bullshit notion of salvation—but the only one who needs saving is you." He put his hand on his belt. "Now bring your crippled ass over here before I take a piss on your precious medal."

Everything happened quickly, in bright flashes of color and movement. Donald's gaze flicked to the medal and back as Petrosky loosened his belt. Then Donald lunged, flying from the chair as if there were springs in the seat, clawing and spitting, Roscoe tumbling to the floor and skittering away as Petrosky dropped his belt and sidestepped the man. Donald crashed into the table. The glass box shattered on the floor in a thousand glittering pieces. Donald howled, spittle clinging to his lips, his eyes blazing with fury, but a little treadmill walking couldn't compete with standing all day— Petrosky stuck a leg between Donald's ankles, stepped out of the way again, and watched him sprawl to the floor on his hands and knees. Then he kicked Donald once in the ribs and jammed his knee hard against the man's spine, feeling Donald's arms give out as his belly hit the wood with an *oomph*.

Petrosky reached for his gun, felt the cool kiss of the metal, saw Heather's face in his mind's eye, the tiniest twitch of her lips as she whispered: *Shoot him.*

*I can't.*

Some things you couldn't justify, not when there was a better way. He pulled out his cuffs instead, shoved his knee harder into Donald's back, and listened to the man groan into the hardwood floor as he clanked the metal around Donald's wrists. It had started with handcuff steel, the first bracelet he'd given Heather. It should end with handcuffs too.

From the wall above, Jesus watched them, and Petrosky stared back at the crucifix. *Repent, sinners.* The hypocrisy seeped into his bones. They were all only human: priests, parents, soldiers, his own brothers in blue, all of them flawed in their own way, some sicker than others. Even Father

Norman had left his own daughter with a murderer to protect his reputation. There was no such thing as salvation; this life was the only one you got, and if you fucked up here, you didn't get a second chance.

No one was going to swoop in and save you—just like no one on the force had helped him solve this. From now on, Petrosky'd do things his way, and screw anyone who didn't like it. He'd do it for Heather. For all the forgotten, the women who'd been robbed of a voice because of shitty circumstances or some fucking maniac intent on silencing them—the women who died in vain, ignored and alone, shoved into a drawer with the other cold cases because some asshole detective thought they didn't matter.

Petrosky planted his foot dead center on Donald's back and pulled out his pack of cigarettes. And as the smoke curled around his nostrils, fogging out the rest of the world, his mind felt clearer than it had in years.

*The fuck you want to be, boy?*

*A detective, sir.* Petrosky smiled.

*A detective.*

# EPILOGUE
## FOUR MONTHS LATER

HYACINTH AND APPLE blossoms sweetened the air as Petrosky drove through a quaint neighborhood of little houses and neatly cut grass, a few boarded-up places sprinkled between. But the trees on this road made up for any abandoned structures; pink and white flowers exploded above him. Spring had come late this year, but that was fine. Petrosky hadn't quite felt "springy" lately. It almost seemed wrong for the seasons to change—as if the weather, too, was trying to leave behind the horror of that winter, trying to force Heather's name from his mind. Trying to vanquish her twitchy smile with golden sun.

He slowed, his tires crunching on the limestone as he pulled into a driveway and parked beneath an enormous cherry tree. The sweetness of the blooms hung thick in the air; everything smelled more like blossoms and less like blood these days. His memories of Heather hadn't gone yet, but he hadn't woken up to bloody images in weeks, and the smell of her, the sound of her voice…those things had melted, too, along with the snow. He tried not to feel guilty, told himself he couldn't recall Joey's voice either—some days, it took him several minutes to recall his dead comrade's name. That would surely happen with Heather, too, like it had with every other painful memory—eventually, he'd forget her. For now, forgetting even small pieces of Heather made his heart ache...sometimes. Most days, he just didn't think about it. Couldn't think about it. Not if he wanted to stay above the darkness.

But he did think about Donald. And somehow that assuaged the pain of losing Heather, just a little, enough to make breathing easier. Donald hadn't lied about the cancer that was eating away at his pancreas and probably the rest of him by now. And there was no way the man would ever see the outside of the jail again. The rifle in Don's attic had been a match for the bullet pulled from Marius Brown's chest, and the handgun in Donald's bedside table, the same one used to kill his wife, had also fired the bullet that had injured Patrick. Whether or not they managed to convict him of Heather's murder, he'd die in a cell. Alone.

At least Roscoe had a new home—a far better one.

Petrosky reached for the doorbell, and Roscoe's yip-yip-yipping sounded from inside. The knob turned. The door swung inward.

Linda smiled at him, her hazel eyes crinkling at the corners as Roscoe leapt out onto the porch and put his tiny front paws on Petrosky's shin, tail wagging so hard his entire body wiggled. Petrosky hadn't wanted to take the dog himself, just couldn't do it, but Linda...she'd picked up the slack. Helped him more than anyone else had. Linda knew what it was to grieve—she'd been involved with a firefighter who was killed during an arson investigation. And she'd bounced back.

That gave him hope.

Petrosky knelt and scratched behind Roscoe's ears, and the dog licked his hand so frantically, he fell from Petrosky's leg and landed on his side, then sprung to his feet again. The little dog was far more vibrant now than he had been in Donald's care, and Petrosky had to wonder whether Heather's father had drugged the little pup to keep it still—forcing even his pet to accept his twisted, self-inflicted immobility.

"What the hell are you feeding him?" Petrosky looked up, and Linda leaned against the doorframe and laughed.

"Oh, you know. Little of this…" She shrugged and gestured to the house. "Speaking of…want some coffee?"

"You know I never turn down good coffee." He stood. He'd been drinking a lot more coffee—and a lot less booze—since the chief had started giving him more responsibilities. He hadn't touched whiskey in a month, though he had gone out for a Guinness with his partner. He wasn't a detective yet, but he was on the fast track—bringing Donald in had helped his credibility. Passing the exams had helped more. Even Patrick had put in a good word, then told Petrosky not to slack off because it was time he did his own growing no matter how tall his father was—or some such shit. But the Irishman's recommendation had helped; turned out, being friendly with the brass had its perks.

But Petrosky would leave the friendliness to ol' Paddy.

Linda was still smiling at him. "I can't guarantee the coffee is good, but it's hot."

"As long as it isn't decaf."

"Like that's even coffee." She rolled her eyes and started for the foyer, but turned back. "Thanks for the limestone, by the way." Her gaze softened. "Really took care of the holes in the drive."

"Oh yeah, no problem. I was getting tired of almost breaking a leg every time I came to pet the dog, so…"

"Yeah…I can imagine."

Limestone wasn't a purple coat or even a yellow one, but it was something. Something good.

A rustling sounded above him, and he tipped his face up toward the branches of the cherry tree. A little bird—a gray dove—sat fluttering its wings on one of the lower boughs. It cooed at him.

"You okay?" Linda was looking at him, head cocked.

*What do you want to be, boy?*

*Happy, sir. Happy.*

"Yeah. I'm good." He smiled and followed Linda and Roscoe inside.

---

**Like *Salvation*?
Don't miss any of Detective Petrosky's adventures!
Go to MEGHANOFLYNN.COM for your
copy of *Famished*, the next book in the Ash Park
series, then read on for a sneak peek.**

---

"SMART AND SUSPENSEFUL AND COMPLETELY TWISTED, FULL OF MULTI-DIMENSIONAL CHARACTERS WHO AREN'T ALWAYS ON THE RIGHT SIDE OF GOOD--BUT YOU LOVE THEM ANYWAY. OR LOVE TO HATE THEM."
~BESTSELLING AUTHOR MARY WIDDICKS

# FAMISHED

AN ASH PARK NOVEL

## SUNDAY, DECEMBER 6TH

*FOCUS, or she's dead.*

Petrosky ground his teeth together, but it didn't stop the panic from swelling hot and frantic within him. After the arrest last week, this crime should have been fucking impossible.

He wished it were a copycat. He knew it wasn't.

Anger knotted his chest as he examined the corpse that lay in the middle of the cavernous living room. Dominic Harwick's intestines spilled onto the white marble floor as though someone had tried to run off with them. His eyes were wide, milky at the edges already, so it had been awhile since someone gutted his sorry ass and turned him into a rag doll in a three-thousand-dollar suit.

*That rich prick should have been able to protect her.*

Petrosky looked at the couch: luxurious, empty, cold. Last week Hannah had sat on that couch, staring at him with wide green eyes that made her seem older than her twenty-three years. She had been happy, like Julie had been before she was stolen from him. He pictured Hannah as she might have been at eight years old, skirt twirling, dark hair flying, face flushed with sun, like one of the photos of Julie he kept tucked in his wallet.

They all started so innocent, so pure, so...*vulnerable.*

The idea that Hannah was the catalyst in the deaths of eight others, the cornerstone of some serial killer's plan, had not occurred to him when they first met. But it had later. It did now.

Petrosky resisted the urge to kick the body and refocused on the couch. Crimson congealed along the white leather as if marking Hannah's departure.

He wondered if the blood was hers.

The click of a doorknob caught Petrosky's attention. He turned to see Bryant Graves, the lead FBI agent, entering the room from the garage door, followed by four other agents. Petrosky tried not to think about what might be in the garage. Instead, he watched the four men survey the living room from different angles, their movements practically choreographed.

"Damn, does everyone that girl knows get whacked?" one of the agents asked.

"Pretty much," said another.

A plain-clothed agent stooped to inspect a chunk of scalp on the floor. Whitish-blond hair waved, tentacle-like, from the dead skin, beckoning Petrosky to touch it.

"You know this guy?" one of Graves's cronies asked from the doorway.

"Dominic Harwick." Petrosky nearly spat out the bastard's name.

"No signs of forced entry, so one of them knew the killer," Graves said.

"*She* knew the killer," Petrosky said. "Obsession builds over time. This level of obsession indicates it was probably someone she knew well."

*But who?*

Petrosky turned back to the floor in front of him, where words scrawled in blood had dried sickly brown in the morning light.

> Ever drifting down the stream—
> Lingering in the golden gleam—
> Life, what is it but a dream?

Petrosky's gut clenched. He forced himself to look at Graves. "And, Han—" *Hannah*. Her name caught in his throat, sharp like a razor blade. "The girl?"

"There are bloody drag marks heading out to the back shower and a pile of bloody clothes," Graves said. "He must have cleaned her up before taking her. We've got the techs on it now, but they're working the perimeter first." Graves bent and used a pencil to lift the edge of the scalp, but it was suctioned to the floor with dried blood.

"Hair? That's new," said another voice. Petrosky didn't bother to find out who had spoken. He stared at the coppery stains on the floor, his muscles twitching with anticipation. Someone could be tearing her apart as the agents roped off the room. How long did she have? He wanted to run, to find her, but he had no idea where to look.

"Bag it," Graves said to the agent examining the scalp, then turned to Petrosky. "It's all been connected from the beginning. Either Hannah Montgomery was his target all along or she's just another random victim. I think the fact that she isn't filleted on the floor like the others points to her being the goal, not an extra."

"He's got something special planned for her," Petrosky

whispered. He hung his head, hoping it wasn't already too late.

If it was, it was all his fault.

---

**GET *FAMISHED* AT MEGHANOFLYNN.COM.**

---

"Fearless, smart writing, and a plot that will stick with you."
~Award-winning Author Beth Teliho

# WICKED SHARP

A BORN BAD NOVEL


**A mountain hike with your serial killer father.
Good Samaritans who aren't as innocent as they appear.
What could go wrong?**


## CHAPTER 1


I HAVE a drawing that I keep tucked inside an old doll house —well, a house for fairies. My father always insisted upon the whimsical, albeit in small amounts. It's little quirks like that which make you real to people. Which make you safe. Everyone has some weird thing they cling to in times of stress, whether it's listening to a favorite song or snuggling up in a comfortable blanket or talking to the sky as if it might respond. I had the fairies.

And that little fairy house, now blackened by soot and flame, is as good a place as any to keep the things that should be gone. I haven't looked at the drawing since the day I brought it home, can't even remember stealing it, but I can describe every jagged line by heart.

The crude slashes of black that make up the stick figure's arms, the page torn where the scribbled lines meet—shredded by the pressure of the crayon's point. The sadness of the smallest figure. The horrific, monstrous smile on the father, dead center in the middle of the page.

Looking back, it should have been a warning—I should have known, I should have run. The child who drew it was no longer there to tell me what happened by the time I stumbled into that house. The boy knew too much, that was obvious from the picture.

Children have a way of knowing things that adults don't—a heightened sense of self-preservation that we slowly lose over time as we convince ourselves that the prickling along the backs of our necks is nothing to worry about. Children are too vulnerable not to be ruled by emotion—they're hardwired to identify threats with razor's-edge precision. Unfortunately, they have a limited capacity to describe the perils they uncover. They can't explain why their teacher is scary or what makes them duck into the house if they see the neighbor peeking at them from behind the blinds. They cry. They wet their pants.

They draw pictures of monsters under the bed to process what they can't articulate.

Luckily, most children never find out that the monsters under their bed are real.

I never had that luxury. But even as a child, I was comforted that my father was a bigger, stronger monster than anything outside could ever be. He would protect me. I knew that to be a fact the way other people know the sky is blue or that their racist Uncle Earl is going to fuck up

Thanksgiving. Monster or not, he was my world. And I adored him in the way only a daughter can.

I know that's strange to say—to love a man even if you see what terrors lurk beneath. My therapist says it's normal, but she's prone to sugarcoating. Or maybe she's so good at positive thinking that she's grown blind to real evil.

I'm not sure what she'd say about the drawing in the fairy house. I'm not sure what she'd think about me if I told her that I understood why my father did what he did, not because I thought it was justified, but because I understood him. I'm an expert when it comes to the motivation of the creatures underneath the bed.

And I guess that's why I live where I do, hidden in the New Hampshire wilderness as if I can keep every piece of the past beyond the border of the property—as if a fence might keep the lurking dark from creeping in through the cracks. And there are always cracks, no matter how hard you try to plug them. Humanity is a perilous condition rife with self-inflicted torment and psychological vulnerabilities, the what-ifs and maybes contained only by paper-thin flesh any inch of which is soft enough to puncture if your blade is sharp.

I knew that before I found the picture, of course, but something in those jagged lines of crayon drove it home, or dug it in a little deeper. Something changed that week in the mountains. Something foundational, perhaps the first glimmer of certainty that I'd one day need an escape plan. But though I like to think I was trying to save myself from day one, it's hard to tell through the haze of memory. There are always holes. Cracks.

I don't spend a lot of time reminiscing; I'm not especially nostalgic. I think I lost that little piece of myself first. But I'll never forget the way the sky roiled with electricity, the greenish tinge that threaded through the clouds and seemed to slide down my throat and into my lungs. I can feel the vibration in the air from the birds rising on frantically beating wings. The smell of damp earth and rotting pine will never leave me.

Yes, it was the storm that kept it memorable; it was the mountains.

It was the woman.

It was the blood.

---

**GET *WICKED SHARP* ON MEGHANOFLYNN.COM.**

---

"FULL OF COMPLEX, ENGAGING CHARACTERS AND EVOCATIVE DETAIL, *WICKED SHARP* IS A WHITE-KNUCKLE THRILL RIDE. O'FLYNN IS A MASTER STORYTELLER." ~PAUL AUSTIN ARDOIN, USA TODAY BESTSELLING AUTHOR

# SHADOW'S KEEP

## A NOVEL

For William Shannahan, six thirty on Tuesday, the third of August, was "the moment." Life was full of those moments, his mother had always told him, experiences that prevented you from going back to who you were before, tiny decisions that changed you forever.

And that morning, the moment came and went, though he didn't recognize it, nor would he ever have wished to recall that morning again for as long as he lived. But he would never, from that day on, be able to forget it.

He left his Mississippi farmhouse a little after six, dressed in running shorts and an old T-shirt that still had sunny yellow paint dashed across the front from decorating the child's room. *The child.* William had named him Brett, but he'd never told anyone that. To everyone else, the baby was just that-thing-you-could-never-mention, particularly since William had also lost his wife at Bartlett General.

His green Nikes beat against the gravel, a blunt metronome as he left the porch and started along the road parallel to the Oval, what the townsfolk called the near hundred square miles of woods that had turned marshy wasteland when freeway construction had dammed the creeks downstream. Before William was born, those fifty or so unlucky folks who owned property inside the Oval had gotten some settlement from the developers when their houses flooded and were deemed uninhabitable. Now those homes were part of a ghost town, tucked well beyond the reach of prying eyes.

William's mother had called it a disgrace. William thought it might be the price of progress, though he'd never dared to tell her that. He'd also never told her that his fondest memory of the Oval was when his best friend Mike had beat the crap out of Kevin Pultzer for punching William in the eye. That was before Mike was the sheriff, back when they were all just "us" or "them," and William had always been a them, except when Mike was around. He might fit in somewhere else, some other place where the rest of the dorky goofballs lived, but here in Graybel, he was just a little…odd. Oh well. People in this town gossiped far too much to trust them as friends anyway.

William sniffed at the marshy air, the closely-shorn grass sucking at his sneakers as he increased his pace. Somewhere near him, a bird shrieked, sharp and high. He startled as it took flight above him with another aggravated scream.

Straight ahead, the car road leading into town was bathed in filtered dawn, the first rays of sun painting the gravel gold, though the road was slippery with moss and morning damp. To his right, deep shadows pulled at him from the trees; the tall pines crouched close together as if hiding a secret bundle in their underbrush. Dark but calm, quiet—comforting. Legs pumping, William headed off the road toward the pines.

A snap like that of a muted gunshot echoed through the morning air, somewhere deep inside the wooded stillness, and though it was surely just a fox, or maybe a raccoon, he paused, running in place, disquiet spreading through him like the worms of fog that were only now rolling out from under the trees to be burned off as the sun made its debut. Cops never got a moment off, although in this sleepy town, the worst he'd see today would be an argument over cattle. He glanced up the road. Squinted. Should he continue up the brighter main street or escape into the shadows beneath the trees?

That was his moment.

William ran toward the woods.

As soon as he set foot inside the tree line, the dark descended on him like a blanket, the cool air brushing his face as another hawk shrieked overhead. William nodded to it as if the animal had sought his approval, then swiped his arm over his forehead and dodged a limb, pick-jogging his way down the path. A branch caught his ear. He winced. Six foot three was great for some things, but not for running in the woods. Either that or God was pissed at him, which wouldn't be surprising, though he wasn't clear on what he had done wrong. Probably for smirking at his memories of Kevin Pultzer with a torn T-shirt and a bloodied nose.

He smiled again, just a little one this time.

When the path opened up, he raised his gaze above the canopy. He had an hour before he needed to be at the precinct, but the pewter sky beckoned him to run quicker before the heat crept up. It was a good day to turn forty-two, he decided. He might not be the best-looking guy around, but he had his health. And there was a woman whom he adored, even if she wasn't sure about him yet.

William didn't blame her. He probably didn't deserve her, but he'd surely try to convince her that he did like he had with Marianna...though he didn't think weird card tricks would help this time. But weird was what he had. Without it, he was just background noise, part of the wallpaper of this small town, and at forty-one—*no, forty-two, now*—he was running out of time to start over.

He was pondering this when he rounded the bend and saw the feet. Pale soles barely bigger than his hand, poking from behind a rust-colored boulder that sat a few feet from the edge of the trail. He stopped, his heart throbbing an erratic rhythm in his ears.

*Please let it be a doll.* But he saw the flies buzzing around the top of the boulder. Buzzing. Buzzing.

William crept forward along the path, reaching for his hip where his gun usually sat, but he touched only cloth. The dried yellow paint scratched his thumb. He thrust his hand into his pocket for his lucky coin. No quarter. Only his phone.

William approached the rock, the edges of his vision dark and unfocused as if he were looking through a telescope, but in the dirt around the stone, he could make out deep paw prints. Probably from a dog or a coyote, though these were *enormous*—nearly the size of a salad plate, too big for anything he'd expect to find in these woods. He frantically scanned the underbrush, trying to locate the animal, but saw only a cardinal appraising him from a nearby branch.

*Someone's back there, someone needs my help.*

He stepped closer to the boulder. *Please don't let it be what I think it is.* Two more steps and he'd be able to see beyond the rock, but he could not drag his gaze from the trees where he was certain canine eyes were watching. Still, nothing there save the shaded bark of the surrounding woods. He took another step—cold oozed from the muddy earth into his shoe and around his left ankle like a hand from the grave. William stumbled, pulling his gaze from the trees just in time to see the boulder rushing at his head, and then he was on his side in the slimy filth to the right of the boulder next to...

*Oh god, oh god, oh god.*

William had seen death in his twenty years as a deputy, but usually it was the result of a drunken accident, a car wreck, an old man found dead on his couch.

This was not that. The boy was no more than six, probably less. He lay on a carpet of rotting leaves, one arm draped over his chest, legs splayed haphazardly as if he, too, had tripped in the muck. But this wasn't an accident; the boy's throat was torn, jagged ribbons of flesh peeled back, drooping on either side of the muscle meat, the unwanted skin on a Thanksgiving turkey. Deep gouges permeated his chest and abdomen, black slashes against mottled green flesh, the wounds obscured behind his shredded clothing and bits of twigs and leaves.

William scrambled backward, clawing at the ground, his muddy shoe kicking the child's ruined calf, where the boy's shy white bones peeked from under congealing blackish tissue. The legs looked...*chewed on.*

His hand slipped in the muck. The child's face was turned to his, mouth open, black tongue lolling as if he were about to plead for help. *Not good, oh shit, not good.*

William finally clambered to standing, yanked his cell from his pocket, and tapped a button, barely registering his friend's answering bark. A fly lit on the boy's eyebrow above a single white mushroom that crept upward over the landscape of his cheek, rooted in the empty socket that had once contained an eye.

"Mike, it's William. I need a... Tell Dr. Klinger to bring the wagon."

He stepped backward, toward the path, shoe sinking again, the mud trying to root him there, and he yanked his foot free with a squelching sound. Another step backward, and he was on the path, and another step off the path again, and another, another, feet moving until his back slammed against a gnarled oak on the opposite side of the trail. He jerked his head up, squinting through the greening awning half convinced the boy's assailant would be perched there, ready to leap from the trees and lurch him into oblivion on flensing jaws. But there was no wretched animal. Blue leaked through the filtered haze of dawn.

William lowered his gaze, Mike's voice a distant crackle irritating the edges of his brain but not breaking through—he could not understand what his friend was saying. He stopped trying to decipher it and said, "I'm on the trails behind my house, found a body. Tell them to come in through the path on the Winchester side." He tried to listen to the receiver but heard only the buzzing of flies across the trail—had they been so loud a moment ago? Their noise grew, amplified to unnatural volumes, filling his head until every other sound fell away—was Mike still talking? He pushed *End,* pocketed the phone, and then leaned back and slid down the tree trunk.

And William Shannahan, not recognizing the event the rest of his life would hinge upon, sat at the base of a gnarled oak tree on Tuesday, the third of August, put his head into his hands, and wept.

---

**GET *SHADOW'S KEEP* AT MEGHANOFLYNN.COM.**

---

"MASTERFUL, STAGGERING, TWISTED... AND
COMPLETELY UNPREDICTABLE."
~BESTSELLING AUTHOR WENDY HEARD

# ABOUT THE AUTHOR

With books deemed "visceral, haunting, and fully immersive" (*New York Times bestseller, Andra Watkins*), Meghan O'Flynn has made her mark on the thriller genre. Meghan is a clinical therapist who draws her character inspiration from her knowledge of the human psyche. She is the bestselling author of gritty crime novels and serial killer thrillers, all of which take readers on the dark, gripping, and unputdown-able journey for which Meghan is notorious. Learn more at https://meghanoflynn.com! While you're there, join Meghan's reader group, and get a **FREE SHORT STORY** just for signing up.

**Want to connect with Meghan?**
**https://meghanoflynn.com**